MRS. MARTIN'S INCOMPARABLE ADVENTURE

COURTNEY MILAN

For Yuzuru Hanyu—
the eternal proof that not all men

also a very good source of calming videos
(again the sea of flags from Japan—
what can he produce lying in fifth place?)

CHAPTER ONE

Surrey County, England, late autumn, 1867

Miss Violetta Beauchamps had made a terrible mistake. It wasn't the taxing journey from London. Nor was it the coin she'd spent—money she could ill afford—on hiring a cart to come to this large country house that belonged to one Mrs. Martin. Waiting in the parlor for half an hour with her doubts eating away at her certainty had not been a mistake, even though she had spent the entire time wondering if the reason she'd not been offered tea or refreshments was because the target already knew the truth.

No. She was beginning to think this entire scheme had been a very bad idea.

Well. Technically, she had *known* it was a bad idea the moment it came to mind. It had just been the best bad idea out of a truly rotten lot. She should apologize. She should go. She should—

She heard steps behind her, finally, and her circling thoughts fled like a flock of geese rising from a pond at the crack of a shot. She stood slowly, her back cracking audibly as she did.

1

"Well? What do you want?" The woman who came into the parlor did not look the way Violetta had imagined. She'd expected someone around her age, but stuffier in every regard—her hair, her gown, her corset, her manners. The woman who stood in the doorway had hair of pale white, tugged up into an unpretentious bun. She wore a loose, pink gown, probably silk—comfortable and opulent all at the same time.

Violetta had done her research. She always did. Mrs. Martin owned this massive home and had a fortune in the tens of thousands of pounds stashed in the five percents. Apparently all that money wasn't enough for her to purchase a little politeness. This comfortable woman had the gall to demand what *Violetta* wanted, without so much as an introduction or an exchange of polite talk?

True, Violetta was here to swindle the woman. But Mrs. Martin didn't know that yet.

Violetta considered her options before inclining her head. "And how do you do? You must be Mrs. Martin. I am Miss Violetta Beauchamps, up from London. I hope your morning has been going well."

Mrs. Martin's nose wrinkled at these pleasantries. She acted as if Violetta were some sort of an interloper.

Violetta was not just *some* sort of interloper—she was the worst sort. She was here to put one over on this woman. But from what she had seen of the massive house, Mrs. Martin wouldn't miss what little Violetta would take, not in the slightest.

Mrs. Martin continued the conversation as she had begun it—with an unpleasant huff. "Blah blah blah," she said. "Imagine I just uttered all the greetings that politeness requires. What do you want? Answer *now,* truthfully, or get out."

What did Violetta want? She wanted not to starve. Moralists would undoubtedly tell her that it was too early to turn to crime out of desperation. She knew this; she had done the calculations (impeccably, perfectly—as always) for two nights running. She had spent all her life being careful, and she would not run through her savings for another five years, if she were frugal. She might—perhaps—at the age of sixty-nine find gainful employment once again, at a comfortable wage that allowed her to put aside a small sum on a monthly basis.

Just because she'd never been struck by extraordinary luck before didn't mean it couldn't happen.

The woman hadn't invited her to sit, but then again, Mrs. Martin had told her to imagine whatever pleasantries she wanted. She sank back onto the white and gold damask sofa in this fussy parlor and pinched the bridge of her nose.

Violetta had not made it to this age with the pleasant fortune of having fifty-seven pounds in the bank, with no debts, without being excessively practical.

Mrs. Martin was pretty in the way that conventional, comfortable women often were. She came and sat opposite Violetta with something near perfect posture. Of course. She had no burdens weighing down her shoulders. She had no fears dragging at her future. Her head was held high; her neck was long and graceful.

Violetta had never been pretty, not at any age. She'd always been too round, and one of her eyes had never moved as it ought—"it's disconcerting," a man had told her once. "It's unnatural."

She'd learned not to look at people directly.

Now that she was older, she was even less exciting. Everyone wished she would disappear, and she would be happy to fade into the background so long as she had enough to eat for the rest of her life, thank you.

Nobody was going to hire her again—not for the wage she was used to earning, at any rate. She was sixty-nine and unmarried—one of the so-called *surplus women* who choked up the attics and rooming houses of London. Never mind her experience, her meticulous calculational capabilities, her voluminous memory. She was old and unpretty, and she could either scrape and grow more and more desperate as the years passed…or she could do *this*.

All she had to do was tell one lie. Everything else would be God's honest truth. *One* lie, and if it was believed, she'd be able to spend the rest of her days in her comfortable room, taking nice walks in the park and enjoying the sunshine when it came.

One lie, and she'd have all of that, instead of a slow slide into desperation.

She started with that one lie: "I am here on a matter of business. I own a rooming house in London."

She did *not* own the rooming house in question; she had managed it for Mr. Toggert and his father and grandfather before him for forty-seven years, along with twelve of his other properties. She'd made them a reasonable sum of money. For decades, the reigning Toggerts had praised her diligence, her book-keeping, her careful work. The latest Mr. Toggert had promised her a pension if she worked for him until she was seventy.

He'd sacked her two days ago, eleven months shy of that goal.

Mrs. Martin rolled her eyes, looking singularly unimpressed. "Good for you. I hope you like it."

Violetta pressed on. "I rent rooms to several men, including—"

"Well," interrupted Mrs. Martin. "There's your problem, right there. I have no idea what cocka-mamie story you're about to tell me, but *don't* rent rooms to men. They get drunk, piss in the corner, and who knows what else? If you'd desist in that one thing, I'm certain your life would improve im-mensely. There. Problem solved. Are we finished?"

In Violetta's forty-seven years managing Mr. Toggert's rooming houses, men had done every single one of those things. Monthly. She fixed her face in a smile. "Allow me to explain. One of the men who has taken a set of rooms in my house is Robert Cappish."

The look on Mrs. Martin's face changed from an-noyed to something far worse. Her nose wrinkled. Her eyes rolled. She looked upward and shook her head.

"Well," she said after a moment. "That's an even worse problem. You have my sincerest condolences on your lack of intelligence in letting rooms to what has to be the worst specimen of humanity on the planet. We do not use that name around here, I am sorry to say. If you must refer to him, you may call him the 'Terrible Nephew.'"

Violetta had not wanted to lease the room to him at all. She had wanted him tossed out *years* ago. Mr. Toggert had insisted. "He has not paid a penny in twenty-seven months."

"That's because he doesn't have any money," Mrs. Martin replied. "He did his best to spend his mother's allowance when she was alive. After she passed away a decade ago, he ran through his inheritance in a matter of five years, and my patience two years after that. Throw him out on the street. Sell his belongings. Salt the earth behind him as he leaves. What on earth has taken you so long?"

Mr. Toggert had said that if they pressed the matter, they would lose his custom, which would be considerable once Mr. Cappish came into his inheritance. The current Mr. Toggert had insisted they wait, and only make occasional gentle inquiries. Then he had demanded to know why his profits had gone down. Violetta had explained that it had been *his* decisions that had led to the result, but he hadn't listened. He had sacked her.

She had realized, watching his eyes glaze through her careful explanation, that it had all been a pretext. He had *wanted* to sack her and avoid the pension. He'd created the excuse to do so.

"Mr. Cap—" Violetta caught herself at the other woman's ferocious glower. "Your, ah, Terrible Nephew claims you will pay on his behalf."

"He lies." Mrs. Martin sighed. "He is very good at that, you know. I have far more experience denying his creditors than you have in collecting, I am certain."

"But when we let him the rooms, you signed as surety."

"I would never have done so. That was also a lie."

Violetta had never considered this possibility. It had seemed so perfect, the opportunity. Still, she could not give in so easily.

"But..." She leaned down and found her bag at her feet, and withdrew the file she had stolen before she left Mr. Toggert's office that final time. She had a record of payments (few); here, a copy of the lease, signed in Mr. Cappish's own hand. And there...

"Here." She held out the sheet. "This is your signature, agreeing to pay the amount in question if he fails to do so."

"That's not my signature," Mrs. Martin shot back. She stood, waved a maid forward, and—when the woman returned a half minute later with a lap desk—scrawled lazily along a sheet of paper. "That's my signature." She folded her arms. "My Christian name is spelled Bertrice. B-E-R-T-R-I-C-E, not B-E-R-T-E-R-I-C-E. I know how to spell my own name. My idiot of a Terrible Nephew does not."

"But—"

"He forged it, I'm sure," Mrs. Martin said. "He does that. He can't be trusted. Not at all. He truly is terrible. A little forgery is the mildest of his crimes."

Drat. Her plan had seemed so simple—go to Mrs. Martin, apologetically demand payment for the two and a half years due, collect almost seventy pounds, and then disappear with her ill-gotten gains.

Was it a crime?

Yes.

But it should *also* have been a crime to promise a woman a pension and then—after forty-seven years of service—sack her eleven months before the pension came due, for doing precisely what you'd made her do under protest. Two wrongs didn't make a right, but occasionally they did make an escape.

There was nothing for her to do but beg.

She bowed her head before Mrs. Martin. "I am sorry. I ought to have been more zealous in looking over matters."

Mrs. Martin blinked, her eyes narrowing in suspicion. "Why are you apologizing to me?"

"I know you have no obligation to me," Violetta continued, "but I implore you. You cannot leave me with this man in my rooming house, his debts unpaid. I'm old."

"You're not old. You're my age."

"I'm sixty-nine," Violetta said. "I'm weaker than

7

him physically, and I have no way to press the matter, not without risking my own safety. The proceeds from the rooming house are my only income. I beg you, woman to woman. Please help me." She bowed her head. She could hear the hint of her own very real desperation peeking out in the quaver of her voice, and she hoped it would be convincing.

Silence.

Silence was heartening, because Mrs. Martin was not immediately rejecting the idea. She had been blunt enough throughout the conversation; Violetta had no doubt that she'd have scoffed immediately if she were entirely unmoved.

Instead, Mrs. Martin reached out and picked up the file. Violetta's meticulous marks marched down that that first sheet, indicating when he'd paid (the first three months only) and what he'd done thereafter. She'd left little notations of conversations after every encounter.

"Hmph." Mrs. Martin tapped one such notation. "This sounds very like him."

Every month, she'd tallied the amount owing. Interest had been added; the sum had grown larger and larger.

Mrs. Martin flipped to the last page, to that final sum. A little more than sixty-eight pounds. It would be enough to save Violetta.

"You want me to pay *this?*" she asked.

"Please."

Mrs. Martin looked up. "It's such a shame. I have vowed that my Terrible Nephew will never get a single penny of mine, not in any way. You cannot imagine the depths of hatred that I harbor for him. He is a wandering fleshbag of fetid morals, and I would rather encase every penny I have in pig manure and toss it into London

Harbor than allow him to have the benefit of a single coin."

"But…"

Mrs. Martin raised a hand. "Give me a moment."

She stood. She straightened, grimacing as she did so, and then leaned on a walking stick. After a moment, her face smoothed.

She left the room with scarcely a limp.

Two minutes later, a maid brought in the refreshments that politeness and hospitality demanded should have provided long before. She laid it all out from a tray—tea and biscuits and sandwiches. For one ridiculous moment, Violetta imagined herself swiping the sugar biscuits into her bag. It had been so long since she had anything sweet at all. Instead, she took one and bit off a corner and let the rich, buttery sweetness dissolve on her tongue.

If *she* had Mrs. Martin's money, there would be biscuits every day.

God. If only she did.

Mrs. Martin returned a few minutes later, sitting herself across from Violetta.

"Sarah," she said, "the ink and paper, please." The maid—who had been standing in the corner since serving refreshments—retrieved the lap desk from where it had been set earlier, removed a pen and a creamy sheet of paper, and set these in front of Mrs. Martin.

Mrs. Martin dipped the pen, a lovely thing of bottle-green, the sort that expensive stores displayed in windows to entice people to enter, and unceremoniously tapped it against the inkwell.

"I have decided that I will do you a favor, Mrs…. What did you say your name was again?"

"Miss," Violetta corrected. "I am Miss Violetta Beauchamps."

Mrs. Martin started writing.

"'I, Mrs. Bertrice Martin'—note the correct spelling."

She pointed at the page, and Violetta nodded.

"'I, Mrs. Bertrice Martin, do agree to use my best efforts to remove—'" Another frown, and she looked up. "Dear God, if this is to be a legal document, I suppose I must use the Terrible Nephew's actual name." She spoke in a way that practically enunciated the capitals. "What do you think?"

Violetta had no idea what was happening. "Perhaps you could soften the effect by using a sufficient number of adjectives?"

"Mmm. Adjectives. I like the way you think. Where was I? Ah, yes. '...my best efforts to remove the despicable, detestable, disgusting—'" She frowned. "That's not enough, gah, my aging brain—"

"Putrid," Violetta suggested. "Loathsome. Slimy. Beastly."

"Excellent. All of those," Mrs. Martin said, scribbling hastily, "but not beastly. I prefer the company of beasts to men."

"Insect-like?"

"Unfair to crickets."

"Vile, then."

"That will have to do. '...slimy, vile Robert Cappish (hereinafter "said Terrible Nephew") from Miss Violetta Beauchamps's property. In exchange, Miss Violetta Beauchamps agrees to never allow said Terrible Nephew to lease one of her rooms again, and to assist in such efforts to remove said Terrible Nephew as requested.'"

That was all well and good, but Violetta needed money. She licked her lips.

Mrs. Martin just looked at her and nodded once, before bending over the paper once more. "'If I am successful in this aim,'" she narrated, "'I promise to give Miss Beauchamps the sum of sixty-eight pounds and 12 shillings for her service, such amount *not* to be accredited to said Terrible Nephew's account because dear God that idiot needs to pay his debts like an actual human being instead of lying like a snake.'" She wrote this out as she spoke.

"Should we be using words like 'idiot' and 'vile' in a legal contract?" Violetta mused. "It seems a bit improper."

"Ah, well." Mrs. Martin frowned at the page. "Maybe you have a point? I don't know. Perhaps as long as we make it clear it's intended to be legal—like this. 'Hereby signed, Mrs. Bertrice Martin.'" She scrawled her signature across the page, then gestured the maid over. "Sarah, you'll witness. The 'hereby' makes it more legalistic, don't you think?"

Violetta was not sure of that. She was not sure about *any* of this. Honestly, she had just hoped for a handful of bills hastily shoved her way. How was she supposed to get the Terrible Nephew to vacate the premises, when she lacked that authority? That would make this *two* crimes, not just one.

But on the other hand… If Mr. Toggert never found out why the Terrible Nephew left…?

It was almost the perfect fraud. Mrs. Martin wasn't asking for his account to be credited; she *insisted* on not doing so, in fact. So the Terrible Nephew would still owe Mr. Toggert the money.

And Mr. Toggert rarely paid attention to his properties. He had not yet hired her replacement; he might not yet for another week. By the time he realized what had happened—and he might never know—Violetta would be long gone, the money with her.

If all went well, Violetta would get something

very like her pension and nobody would ever realize that she'd cheated for every penny of it.

She picked up the pen. "Hereby signed," she intoned, "Violetta Beauchamps."

A moment too late, she realized that perhaps she ought not to have signed her actual, legal name to a crime. Ah, well. Some criminal she made. Good thing she wasn't planning to make a habit of this.

She looked over to see Mrs. Martin smiling.

"This is good," Mrs. Martin said. "My physician said I should embark on an adventure. He suggested Bath. Boring. This is much better. I cannot imagine anything more exhilarating and adventurous than making the Terrible Nephew less comfortable in his surroundings. Let's get started, shall we? I can't wait."

CHAPTER TWO

London, early the next day

I t was horribly anticlimactic for Bertrice Martin to be standing at her Terrible Nephew's door after having knocked, then waited, and then knocked again. She had built up what was to come in her mind for hours. She felt excitement, yes. Anticipation, definitely. Nerves? Those were old friends, especially when it came to standing up to men.

Her stomach churned with a mix of both fear and delight. To find no immediate resolution at all? That left her rather out of sorts.

The rooming house was clean and bright with new paper. The walls were freshly scrubbed. The wooden bannisters going up the stairs were polished. It looked like a very nice rooming house. Far too nice for the likes of her Terrible Nephew to enjoy without paying.

Miss Beauchamps had removed a key from her pocket—just the one, Bertrice had noted, not a great ring of keys—and unlocked the door below.

It was a rooming house in a part of town that was *just* on the near side of genteel. Miss Beauchamps had

13

explained on the train down that she let rooms to single gentlemen—often those who served in government or law, but who didn't *need* to labor for their income.

"Ah," Bertrice had remarked. "Important enough that they know their own importance; not important enough that anyone else would know it."

The corner of the proper Miss Beauchamp's mouth had twitched at that, and something in Bertrice had felt an exhilarating sense of adventure spark in her at that hint of a smile.

The woman was a bit of an enigma. She'd said more about her rooming house than about herself.

"See here," Bertrice had said, "when I call my nephew the 'Terrible Nephew'—I really do mean it. He is utterly terrible."

The woman had smoothed her skirts and not met Bertrice's gaze. "I *do* know. He lives in my rooming house."

There had been just that flatness to her tone that made Bertrice think maybe she really *did* know. If the notes of her conversation were accurate, he'd threatened to call the constable on *her* if she tried to collect, and that was just what Miss Beauchamps had been willing to commit to writing in her precise, elegant hand.

So Bertrice had spent the remainder of the journey plotting precisely what she would say to that perambulating bag of male pretension and violence when she first had him in her sights. It was rather taking the wind out of her sails to have to wait for the opportunity.

"Is he really not here?" She peered at the door, but it remained firmly unanswered.

Next to her, Miss Beauchamps looked up at the ceiling. "We shouldn't be surprised. It's evening. He's a man of a certain age. He's not going to be sitting in front of the fireplace doing needlepoint, you know."

Bertrice should have guessed. He would be off, doing… *Things,* she supposed. Horrible things. *Man* things. Her nose wrinkled. "Well, damn it. What do young things of his age do, anyway?"

"You do realize that Mr. Ca—your Terrible Nephew is forty-nine, yes?"

"He *is* my nephew. I was present for his birth. I am aware of his age."

"I am only saying that forty-nine is not young."

"Oh, for God's sake. Forty-nine is *extremely* young. If forty-nine is not young, that would make *me* old, and I am not old. I have reached the age of maturity to which all humans must particularly aspire; to dismiss this pinnacle of perfection as *old age* is to demean all of humankind."

Miss Beauchamps did not look impressed. "But you use a cane. And your knee, it looked as if you were favoring the other leg—"

"That can hardly signify." Bertrice rapped on the door one last time just to be certain. "Very young children have difficulty walking, and knee pain is not limited to the elderly. Why, just the other day I met a delightful young woman of thirty-seven whose pain was worse than mine."

"How could you know whose pain was worse?"

"I am entirely certain," Bertrice said, because she had never found it useful to admit that she had no idea. "And don't distract me with irrelevant questions —where is that godforsaken mobile rat's nest that masquerades as my nephew? Have you any idea?"

Miss Beauchamps sighed. "There are two likely options. Most of the men who take quarters in this rooming house do so because the rooms are pleasant and well-appointed, and because it essentially shares a wall with a gentleman's club known as Glaser's. They are the only two buildings on the street."

Bertrice felt her lip curl up in distaste. "Gentlemen. In a *club*. All squashed together. How odious. I cannot believe it is allowed."

"Of course it is allowed. They make their own rules." After a moment, Miss Beauchamps shrugged. "They make ours, as well. In any event, I see it more in the light of putting all the cockroaches in one jar."

"A salient point." Bertrice wrinkled her nose. "I'm not certain why one needs a jar of cockroaches."

"It's better than having them scattered around the house. I would expect that either your Terrible Nephew would be in attendance at Glaser's, or..." Miss Beauchamps trailed off. "Or," she finished, "he may be in the park."

"The park. Why would he be in the park? It's almost dark. Don't tell me he takes constitutionals for his health. It's hardly his way. He always was the sort to pretend to box for his exercise."

"Ah." Miss Beauchamps's cheeks colored faintly. "That particular park is where the gentlemen of the club find female companionship, should it be wanted."

This was going to take forever if they couldn't use actual words to describe actual things. "Oh. You mean prostitutes frequent it. Stop circumnavigating the conversation. I know what a prostitute is, and so do you. If God didn't intend us to use the words that He made to refer to the people He created, He would have said so."

Miss Beauchamps looked slightly nonplussed. "I'm no lexicographer, but I do not believe God created the English language." Her frown deepened. "Also, most people don't refer to the ladies of the street as God's creations."

"Their mistake." Bertrice gripped her cane and eyed the stairs going down to the street with distrust. Scarcely wide enough, and no fun to navigate at the end of the day. Well, no point waiting; she gingerly started downward. "My husband, God rot his soul, used to bring prostitutes home all the time. After he'd finished with them, I'd serve them tea and double whatever he was paying them."

Miss Beauchamps huffed, sounding faintly outraged at this. Bertrice just concentrated on descending. Down the stairs was harder than up; she had never figured out why. Perhaps it was all in her head, the notion that she might slip. Still, she found herself clutching the rail. She was focused on the descent when Miss Beauchamp's question came from behind her.

"But why would you do that?"

"Why not? It's good sense to be kind to people who are doing work for you." Bertrice didn't think that was so strange a proposition. "It was hard work fucking my husband. Trust me, I should know. *I* certainly didn't want to do it."

She heard Miss Beauchamps slip on the staircase, and turned back to frown at her. "Take care. It's a narrow stair; you mustn't hurt yourself."

She had no idea what the woman muttered in response. By the time they were out in the clear air, though, there was nothing to do except stand in one place, surreptitiously waiting for the deep ache in her knee to subside, and pretend to look about. The sun was setting over the park. No snow here; that was a mercy. Still, it was cold. There was a bit of wind tonight, chilly enough to cut through her combined layers of shawl and thick cape. She pulled her scarf around her neck and hunched over.

She hoped her Terrible Nephew was enjoying

himself. It would make it all the more satisfying when she ruined his peace.

"There," she said, gesturing with her cane to the building next door to the rooming house. "That's it, that's the gentleman's club?"

It was a nondescript building of white stone, obviously scrubbed regularly to keep it looking clean-ish on the outside. The better, she supposed, to hide the man-rot within. A plaque on the wall, unreadable from this distance, gleamed in the last rays of the sunset. Steps rose up to an entrance that was trying to appear imposing. Two solid black wooden doors with carved silver lions-head knockers seemed almost gratuitously masculine.

"You know what they say," Bertrice muttered to herself. "The grander the entrance, the smaller the brain."

Miss Beauchamps coughed beside her. "I've never heard anyone say that."

"You should see a doctor about that cough. Maybe it's the beginnings of consumption. You wouldn't want that, would you?"

"No," said Miss Beauchamps mildly. "I wouldn't."

A pair of men stood in front of this melodramatically mannish edifice, jawing about…who knew what? The hair on their chests, maybe. As she watched, a third man came up and greeted them.

Again, that feeling of anticipation mixed with dread roiled through her. Bertrice rubbed her hands together to try to dispel her unease. "There. That's him." She squinted. "I think?"

"Maybe we should discuss how to—"

Discussions never helped anything; they inevitably ended in people begging Bertrice not to do whatever it was she wanted to do. She would then have to waste good effort ignoring them. Instead, she pretended she hadn't heard and started forward at as much of a march as she could manage with her knee aching in the cold wind.

"—The club treasury will withstand a month, maybe two," one of her Terrible Nephew's undoubtedly equally terrible companions was saying. "We have been entirely understanding thus far, Mr. Cappish, and while we welcome men of your quality and caliber at Glaser's, even if you temporarily find yourself unable to pay your membership dues, we must ask that you stop imbibing liquor on credit. I am certain that—"

Now would be a good time to interrupt. Bertrice raised her cane like a weapon and shook it in the air. "Robby Bobkins," she said, because she had to say *something* to get his attention, and she had called him that when he was a very small child and still had the appearance of sweetness, "are you going into a house of ill repute?"

It was, indeed, her Terrible Nephew engaged in a hushed conversation about how he was no longer allowed to drink for free. He whirled to look at her, knocking his hat off in the process.

Oh, he did not look well. There was a certain sallowness to his face that suggested that he needed to stop drinking for reasons other than his pocketbook.

"Aunt Bertrice." He sounded utterly shocked. "What are you *doing* here?"

The man standing next to him perked up. "Ah. This is the aunt who…" The man paused, trying to figure out a gentlemanly way to inquire when Bertrice intended to kick off this mortal coil, and how much money she planned to leave her Terrible Nephew when she did.

God, being a gentleman must be a colossal bore.

The Terrible Nephew's gaze fell on the woman

who was following Bertrice, and he frowned. "Miss Beauchamps," he said slowly. "What are *you* doing here? And with my aunt?"

Bertrice shook her cane once more. "*We* ask the questions, Robby Bobkins. Nobody cares about you."

Her nephew sighed with a heave of his shoulders and took a step toward her, lowering his voice furtively. "*Please,* Aunt Bertrice. I know your memory is…not as it once was, but I prefer to be addressed as 'Mr. Cappish.' It's my name. 'Robby Bobkins' is just a little infantilizing, don't you think?"

Bertrice frowned at him. "Robby Bobkins, do you actually *support* yourself with gainful employment?"

"Ack!" The Terrible Nephew took two terrible steps forward, clapping his despicable hands over her mouth. Bertrice didn't know everything he did with them, but she knew enough. She'd told him to never lay hands on her again after he'd knocked her out of her chair for calling the constable on him.

Not again. She was never going to tolerate being thrown about or silenced again, never, never, *never*— not by him, not by anyone else. She bit his fingers as hard as she could.

"Bleah!" The Terrible Nephew pulled away. He shook his hand and glared reproachfully at her. "Don't *say* such things, Aunt Bertrice," he whispered. "I'm a member of Glaser's. It's a respectable club. The members don't need to *work* for our upkeep—only for the betterment of society. It's one of our hallmarks. They'd toss me out if they believed I would be compelled to do such a thing."

"Well." She collected the taste of his vile flesh from between her teeth and spat on the ground. "*I'm* not the one infantilizing you, Robby Bobkins. I can't help it if you're an infant."

He sighed. "Do *not.* Call. Me. That. Please."

Bertrice pitched her voice to carry so that everyone nearby could hear. "Did I ask you what you wish to be called, Robby Bobkins?"

Here was the thing about being the wealthy aunt who her Terrible Nephew needed to please: He really could not be too rude to her in public. Even in private, his worst tendencies were somewhat restrained. She did not want to imagine what he did in his blind rages to women who would definitely *not* leave him forty-six thousand pounds.

The Terrible Nephew exhaled slowly and put a hand over his face, and when he removed it, he was sporting a crocodile's smile.

"Gentlemen," he called over his shoulder. "If you would afford me a little privacy to speak with my aunt? This won't take but a moment." He waited until the other two men moved back ten yards before turning back to Bertrice. "Aunt, if you prefer something more friendly, my intimate acquaintances call me 'Cappy.' I would like it if we were friends. We should mend our relationship." He perked up at this. "I think we would do well to apologize to each other."

Apologize? To *him*? First of all, there *was* no apology for what he'd done. Not for any of it. For another…

"Robby Bobkins," she said, enunciating the name and saying it as loudly as she could, "I am not here to mend our relationship. I am here to make your life a living hell. I have revoked the surety you fraudulently signed on my behalf with regards to the rooms you are letting. You will therefore agree to vacate your living quarters. Immediately."

Her Terrible Nephew's gaze flicked behind her to Miss Beauchamps. "Oh," he said idly, "that's not necessary. Miss Beauchamps won't have me tossed out on the streets."

Bertrice's gaze darted to Miss Beauchamps behind her. They hadn't talked nearly enough. But the woman had struck her as quiet—sturdy and capable, yes, but proper.

It had been a mistake not to make sure they were in full agreement. Miss Beauchamps might be *too* proper. A man with ill intent could easily break a proper woman. The way the Terrible Nephew spoke, it sounded as if he'd reached an agreement with Miss Beauchamps before, and he thought he could make her back down again.

They *should* have talked more, the two of them. The hairs on Bertrice's neck stood on end.

For a second, Miss Beauchamps looked at the pavement, and a disagreeable smile passed over her Terrible Nephew's face.

Then Miss Beauchamps looked up. Her spine straightened. Her jaw squared, and she looked as if she needed only a sword of fire to make her an angel intent on justice.

Up until that moment, Bertrice hadn't realized. It had been so long—too long, really. Since Ellie had passed away a few years back and she'd fallen into a dark malaise.

But looking at Miss Beauchamps with her chin rising an inch and the last light of the sun reflecting on her eyes, Bertrice remembered all of a sudden what it was to want.

She'd spent all her life learning to stand up for herself. She'd learned to tell her husband no, and to mean it. She'd told the Terrible Nephew to go to hell some years ago, the day he'd broken her heart for the final time, when she'd had to admit to herself that he wouldn't change and nothing would bring back the child she'd loved. She'd been the one to stand up for Ellie when she discovered her accountant was swindling her. Bertrice was *good* at standing up. She was used to it.

She hadn't realized she wanted someone to stand up beside her until Miss Beauchamps did so. And maybe all the other woman wanted was the sixty-something pounds she'd been promised, but in that moment, when she decided to step forward, she seemed glorious in the most electrifying way.

"It seems," Miss Beauchamps said, with a quiet determination, "that you don't know Miss Beauchamps as well as you should."

~

When Violetta had signed that perfidious contract with Mrs. Martin, she had imagined standing in the background with her arms folded, nodding sagely, and collecting her money that same day.

She had imagined that Mrs. Martin would command Mr. Cappish's respect in a way that Violetta herself never had. So when he laughed off his aunt's statements and fixed his gaze on Violetta instead, her first response was to panic and drop her eyes, to hope that he'd look through her as if she weren't present, the way men always did.

Her second response was anger—anger that he'd always looked through her, anger that she'd spent her entire life being transparent. She'd been a blur in the background, as uninteresting as a lime wash applied to the wall.

She was *tired* of not existing except as a tool to be brought out when needed. She'd spent all seven decades of her life saying *yes, sir, if you say, sir, I'll see to it, sir.*

But she wasn't an echo. She was a *person*, and if

she was going to sign her full, legal name to a perfidious contract, she was going to fulfill its terms in their entirety.

Violetta's heart pounded. Her skin felt clammy, but she raised her head and looked at the spot just behind Mr. Cappish's head. "Won't she?" Her voice sounded braver than she felt. "*Won't* she have you tossed out on the streets?"

Mr. Cappish's eyes widened. He took a step toward her. He was tall, and at forty-nine, he was indeed young—young enough that he'd lost none of his height. The bulk of him was appallingly imposing, and he knew it. He knew how intimidating it was when he stood less than a hand's width from her. He towered over her and let his voice drop to a low growl.

"You may recall." He gestured behind him. "I'm a member of Glaser's, the renowned gentleman's club that stands as an edifice to all things manly. We are the ninth most renowned gentleman's club in London."

His performance should have sent a chill down her spine. Instead, the earnestness of his voice coupled with the reverence with which he spoke those words struck her as truly amusing.

She couldn't help herself. A snicker escaped Violetta's lips.

Mr. Cappish turned faintly pink. "That other list does *not* count. Imagine ranking Glaser's—*Glaser's,* which has been in continuous operation for seventy-two years—beneath those upstarts at Smith's. It's an *insult* to even think of us at number twelve in London. An absolute *insult.*" He looked at Violetta and gave her a firm nod, as if he had made a salient point.

Violetta almost backed down. She would have done; she *had* done, so many times before.

If she'd owned the rooming house. If she had still worked for Mr. Toggert. If she were not so desperate, and this contract made of lies her only hope. Any number of ifs, and she might have been intimidated.

Instead, she decided to emulate Mrs. Martin—just a little.

"So?" she asked loudly. "Are you trying to make a point? Is it that the gentlemen's clubs numbered one through eight wouldn't have you?"

"That's—" He sputtered. "That's not—dear God, of course I prefer the company at Glaser's! The gentlemen of Glaser's are renowned for their chivalry—"

"The chivalry of threatening two elderly women?" Mrs. Martin tsked next to him. "My, my, Robby Bobkins, what a *fine*, good specimen of manhood you've grown into, able to vanquish two aging ladies with no assistance but the four dozen men who you pay to call themselves your friends."

Violetta felt almost jealous just hearing that speech. It was so delightfully *cutting*. Why couldn't *she* think of insults like that?

"Careful." The Terrible Nephew raised a finger. "I wouldn't insult the men of Glaser's. We are powerful men, friends, dedicated to one another's mutual interest in all matters. Toss me out of your rooming house, and we will personally make your life miserable in ways that you cannot now imagine." He lowered his voice further, and leaned in to whisper in Violetta's ear. "I don't know what you've told my aunt, you old hag, but—"

"There is nothing wrong with my hearing," Mrs. Martin shouted. "How dare you threaten a lady older than you, you villain? For that, Robby Bobkins, you'll pay. I'll make sure of it."

Mr. Cappish just cast an indulgent look at his aunt. "You'll come around, Aunt Bertrice," he said.

"I'm your only living flesh and blood. I'm your beloved sister's only son."

A look passed over Mrs. Martin's face—one that spoke of sadness and loss. She looked away.

Mr. Cappish straightened as if he knew he'd landed a hit.

"Her *only* son," he repeated, "and I know you promised her when she passed away that you would look after me."

Mrs. Martin swallowed, and Violetta felt her hopes of a swift resolution and a tidy addition to her self-funded pension slipping away. It wasn't as if she could enforce the contract she'd signed in Mrs. Martin's living room. What was she to do, go to a magistrate and demand reparations on account of the rooming house she demonstrably did not own?

"There's nothing that's gone wrong between us that we can't fix," Mr. Cappish said gently. "I'm sorry I treated your home with so little respect. See? Apologies are easy. Now, you say that you're sorry, too. My mother would want you to do it. For her, don't you think you can?"

Mrs. Martin exhaled slowly. "I miss her, too."

"I know, Aunt."

"I did promise her that I would do my best to stand in her shoes."

"There, there." Mr. Cappish smiled in satisfaction.

"So I will. Mabel Topham raised us, both of us," Mrs. Martin said. Her chin came up. "She was just a nanny, you might say, but she wasn't. We grew up alongside Sarah Topham." Her eyes lit, blue and fierce, ready to shoot fire. "She was like a sister to both of us. And Sarah's daughter, Lily. She was taking a course on shorthand while she was helping me along, and you—you utter useless cad—you came to my house and you didn't disrespect the damn *build-*

ing, you unthinking pile of fetid refuse. She wanted nothing to do with you, and you tried to rape her." Mrs. Martin stopped, her chin working. "I didn't want to see it. I avoided the possibility for years. I kept hoping I was wrong. But you showed your colors, and I'm glad my sister didn't live to see what you've become."

Violetta felt her stomach turn. God; she'd known that there was something wrong between the two of them. She hadn't known it was *this.*

"Aunt. Those words are so harsh. I've asked you again and again to see my side of it. I'm a *gentleman.* It wasn't rape; I would have paid her afterward. You've been sheltered; you don't know how these things work."

"I know exactly how they work," Mrs. Martin said. "I have money. You have none. I will make your life a misery. I *promise* I will." She raised her voice even more loudly. "Gentlemen, toss this man out of your club. He'll get nothing from me. He'll never repay what he owes your coffers."

"Aunt Bertrice." The Terrible Nephew winced. "You don't *mean* that. I know you won't leave me with nothing. How will I survive?"

"Gainful employment is what most men in your shoes would consider."

Mr. Cappish made his voice a harsh whisper. "That's the second time you've mentioned it. I almost think you're serious, but you *can't possibly* be. Don't make such indelicate jokes around my friends. I know you're just teasing, but what will they think of me? It's one thing to work to fill your hours or to do good, but they must not hear you suggest that I *need* to perform actual labor in exchange for money. How crassly middle-class they would think me!"

"You hear that, gentlemen?" Mrs. Martin announced. "Robby Bobkins here needs to start earning wages for his labor."

"Aunt." He flushed and waved his hands, then turned back. "She's…quite old," he said to his friends who were looking at him from a distance with something like dawning horror. "We should respect her. Even if she's in her cups!"

"Go." She waved her hand in dismissal. "I see you need time to understand your changed circumstances. Go speak this over with your…friends. We'll talk in the morning."

Violetta watched Mr. Cappish retreat into the edifice of Glaser's. She sighed and turned to Mrs. Martin. "The morning? What will you do now? Had you planned to stay overnight?"

"Hmm." Mrs. Martin blinked, looking around at the darkening sky. "Well. I hadn't thought that far in advance. I'm here on doctor's orders, after all. I suppose that I must extend my trip." She frowned, considering. "I'll send for some of my things. See my solicitor, talk to my man-of-affairs, arrange for funds…"

"Where will you be staying?" Violetta racked her brains, trying to come up with a suitable place for a woman who lived in the sprawling expanse of a house that she'd visited out in the country. She'd never had need to think of London lodgings beyond the ones she managed. "Some hotel, perhaps? I suppose if I think, I would know where to inquire…"

"Perhaps." Mrs. Martin's nose scrunched. "Hotels. They're all likely to be far away, and they're so very large and impersonal. But what else am I to do?" She sighed.

Politeness made Violetta speak up. "Or, alternately…. My room isn't much, but…?"

Mrs. Martin brightened immediately, turning to

Violetta with a smile. And what a smile it was. It lit her from within, making her seem like a bonfire in the cold air.

Do not, Violetta thought. *Do not invite this woman to stay with you. She is rich, and you have nothing. She's pretty, and you are plain. She's clever, and you're nothing but a boring woman with a head for figures.*

You're lying to her, and you don't need to like her any more.

Exactly the lecture she needed.

But Mrs. Martin's eyes were wide and she seemed almost vulnerable. "Oh," she said, as if Violetta's tiny room were a treat better than the fanciest London hotel. "Really?"

No, Violetta wanted to say. *Not really.* "It will be a little cramped," she said instead, "far less than you're used to. I don't have servants. We'll have to make our own dinner. I don't think you'll—"

Like it, she was going to say, but Mrs. Martin clapped her hands together. "I've never made my own dinner! If you wouldn't mind? I *did* want an adventure. And what could be better?"

CHAPTER THREE

The place that Miss Beauchamps led Bertrice to was in a different building altogether, two streets down. The room was on the ground floor, thankfully; the hallway was darker and dingier than the rooming house she owned. Miss Beauchamps removed another, single, different key from her pocket to let herself into a single room.

It was smaller than Bertrice had supposed, and crammed with mismatched furniture—table, chair, rocking chair, and a bed covered with thick blankets.

"Not much," Miss Beauchamps said as they were hanging wraps on a hook, a faint flush that might have been embarrassment on her cheeks. "Most of the furnishings are left over from what the tenants abandoned over the years."

She ushered Bertrice to a rocking chair made plush with padded cushions and popped a kettle on the hearth.

The water had not yet begun to hiss, and Bertrice was already beginning to think she'd made a mistake. She'd imagined...well, *more*. A guest room, perhaps. Miss Beauchamps had said she didn't have servants, but Bertrice had expected at least a charwoman.

From the state of the rooming house that Miss Beauchamps owned, she'd imagined she was rather more comfortable than this.

She hadn't wanted to be a bother, but... Hmm. She made a mental note of a question she needed to put to her solicitors, but since it couldn't be asked at this exact moment, she put it out of her mind.

"I know it's not much," Miss Beauchamps was saying, laying out the tea things, "and if you should want to leave after tea and find that hotel after all—"

"If you're trying to be polite and you want me out of your hair, do just say so," Bertrice interrupted. "These circumlocutions wherein one claims one thing and means another have never made much sense to me. Say what you mean! Indirectness is not my strong point."

"Is that so?" Miss Beauchamps murmured. "How nice to have my suspicions confirmed."

"I like it here," Bertrice told her. "It's cozy."

"No, it's—" Miss Beauchamps looked at her for a moment, before smiling brightly. "Never mind. For a second, I thought you were just being polite."

"And then you realized how ridiculous that sounded. Am I imposing on your kindness? Do you *want* me here?"

Miss Beauchamps looked up, pausing with a spoonful of tea on the way to the teapot. She did not meet Bertrice's eyes. Instead, she looked over her shoulder at some distant point; her eyes crossed slightly as she did.

"I'm used to doing whatever I wish," Bertrice said, "but I'm also used to people telling me to go to the devil if they don't want me about. By contrast, you're one of *those*."

"One of which?"

"One of those *nice* people. You do things you don't want to do all the time, don't you? You're *used* to it."

Miss Beauchamps's eyes widened, then narrowed.

"Go on," Bertrice said. "Spit it out, whatever you're thinking."

"The word for people like me isn't 'nice,'" Miss Beauchamps said. "It is 'not massively wealthy.' What you call 'doing things I don't want to' is what the rest of the world calls 'earning a living.' You lectured your nephew about it. You should recognize it."

"Oh." Bertrice blinked. "Oh. But I'm not employing you."

"We have a contract in which I have agreed to do a thing for you, and you have agreed to give me money for doing it, signed with herebys and everything."

So they did. Bertrice hadn't considered. It was less than a hundred pounds, scarcely anything compared to the chance to seek revenge on her nephew.

"I don't mind having you here," Miss Beauchamps said with a sigh. "I'm just embarrassed because my best is so far beneath your worst."

Bertrice sighed and stretched, rubbing her knee. "Don't be so sure. I've been very down recently. I'm actually fawningly grateful to you for rescuing me."

"Rescuing you from...?" The other woman frowned. "From your china and your tea and your servants? I would *love* to be burdened by your wealth. Do you know what I could *do* with it?"

"Have a perpetual stream of charlatans and liars attempt to remove it from you?"

Miss Beauchamps flushed and rearranged the teaspoons in front of her.

"I know," Bertrice said. "It's rude to complain about my enormous wealth. But I honestly forgot I was paying you. I've felt like there was nothing I could do about that weasel of a blood relation, and then you arrived. I'm grateful, that's all."

"Grateful." Miss Beauchamps stared at her spoons a little longer, before shaking her head and turning to the side. She took out a knife from a box and a half-loaf of bread from another. "Grateful," she repeated, cutting thick, perfect slices. She swept the crumbs into a napkin, and then found some cheese. "*Grateful.* Well, I suppose I'll let go of my petty jealousy then."

"I'll give you a fortune; you can see how you like it," Bertrice said.

Miss Beauchamps took this for a joke. "It's not just the money," she said. "I'm—how did you put it? I'm *nice.* At least, I do what people want. I don't make trouble. I've been doing it all my life, and I'm used to it." She seemed to catch herself, shaking her head and slicing cheese. "You say whatever you want, and I feel like I'm always screaming, deep inside where nobody can hear what I'm doing. It's become so bad that I'm afraid I might start doing it out loud."

Oh.

Miss Beauchamps set down the knife and squeezed her eyes together. "But enough about me. If you're going to stay here, I need to know something about you."

Yes, Bertrice thought, *I like women. Once I thought I liked men, too, but I had that burned out of me.*

"Your doctor. You said he suggested this." Miss Beauchamps gathered up the now-sliced bread and cheese and went to the stool near the fire. There was some contraption she had—a metal box of sorts, fire-blackened, with a wooden handle—which she manipulated with practiced ease, sliding the cheese inside. "Are you on the verge of dying? If you collapse, who should I fetch? What should I tell them?"

She sounded so matter-of-fact about the possibility of Bertrice keeling over that Bertrice wanted to laugh. Of *course* that comment about her doctor would sound dire to her. Technically, it would sound dire to everyone.

"It's nothing like that. He says I'll live decades longer. The problem is more that there's no joy in anything. Nothing tastes good. I scarcely want to get out of bed most days. He said that I should go on an adventure. He suggested taking the waters at Bath, but yelling at terrible men is far more restorative, don't you think?"

Miss Beauchamps stopped by the fire, tilting her head, as if considering. After a moment she smiled. "Shockingly so!"

"What are you making?"

"Oh." Miss Beauchamps colored and looked away. "It's nothing much. Just a little toasted cheese with bread for dinner. I have some milk, still. And an apple, of course. An apple a day keeps the doctor away." She frowned. "Well, so does poverty, come to think of it. But that's a bit less healthful."

Mrs. Martin's cook served her bread toasted in thinly sliced points. She'd never watched the woman cut it. She hadn't eaten thick bread with slices of melted cheese since she was a child. She'd certainly never watched another woman swipe hair out of her eyes—dark eyes, deep eyes—and turn a little metal contraption above a coal fire.

"Don't they also say something about toasted cheese?" she asked.

Miss Beauchamps colored. "That those who eat toasted cheese at night will dream of Lucifer?"

"I had not heard of that one!" Bertrice leaned forward. "Is it true?"

"It always struck me as odd that the way to summon Lucifer was to eat poor man's food. The devil doesn't care about poor people any more than Parliament does."

"Oh." Bertrice looked at Miss Beauchamps, and then back at the cheese, then at the fire. Was Miss Beauchamps *poor?* She looked so…proper. But…there was the room. And there was the silent screaming. And there was that desperation over so tiny a sum as seventy-ish pounds.

Oh, dear. Bertrice wasn't much for niceness, but she did care about kindness, and the set of Miss Beauchamps's mouth suggested the other woman did not wish to speak of this any longer.

She changed the subject.

"Won't the cheese melt when you put it over the fire?"

"That's entirely the point."

A few minutes later, Bertrice could hear the cheese snapping inside the metal contraption. She could smell it cooking, salt and savory, and her mouth began to water. A few moments later, her stomach rumbled. It actually *rumbled,* as if she were a mere forty or so years old and hungry for a meal.

It had been so long since she had felt anything like hunger. She had been eating mostly because she was aware that putting food in one's mouth and swallowing it was a thing one was supposed to do if one expected to persist in a living state. She hadn't been hungry.

Her hunger felt like a miracle.

"It's not much," Miss Beauchamps said, maneuvering the cheese onto the bread. She put slices on two tin plates and passed one over to Bertrice. "But I hadn't expected company, and it's all I had."

The cheese was melted through and through. The bottom of the cheese had rested directly on the metal over the fire, and had been browned to a glorious crisp. She'd not been given a knife and fork, but Miss Beauchamps didn't seem to think one was necessary. She just picked up her bread and took one unceremonious bite. Melted cheese spilled over the edge, landing with a plop on her plate.

An adventure. Bertrice lifted her own bread and took a tentative nibble.

Oh. *Oh.*

Maybe it was the fact that the bread was thick enough to be toasted on the outside and still soft in the middle. Maybe it was the cheese. Maybe it was that hint of smoke that the fire had imparted.

Maybe it was that she was watching Miss Beauchamps roll the thick column of her neck, stretching it out.

It was good. It was all so good.

"This toasty cheese thing is so lovely!" she heard herself say.

Miss Beauchamps turned to stare at her.

"It is! I can't remember the last time I enjoyed a good toasty cheese thing."

Maybe it had been back with her sister and Sarah Topham, when they were children sneaking into the kitchen late at night, whispering together and giggling, trying not to wake their nanny.

Food was odd. It awoke memories she'd sworn she had forgotten. Memories of laughter, childhood, friendship…a time before she and her sister had married, when finding a man to tie herself to had been the only care she had in the world. God, it had all seemed so simple back then.

She took another bite. How strange it felt to have an appetite once more. Maybe it was the exertion of the day. Maybe it was the excitement. Maybe it was just the cheese toast.

Miss Beauchamps tentatively smiled at her, and

Bertrice's feelings suddenly clicked into place. That light tickle of interest…she'd felt it since the moment she'd seen Miss Beauchamps in her home back in Surrey. The woman had seemed so proper, so prepared.

Bertrice had stood up for herself again and again, but saying *no* was a reaction, not an identity. Sometimes, it seemed she was nothing but a rejection of other people's demands. For all her certainty, she hadn't had solid moorings in ages. She'd drifted toward Miss Beauchamps—a woman who made perfect cheese toast and told Bertrice precisely what she needed—almost on instinct.

Bertrice had thought about hiring companionship, but she'd stopped letting herself hope for more. How *strange* it felt to have an appetite again. To suddenly find her mind engrossed, wanting details about how someone else's hair was pinned. To wonder about the pink of her lips, to want to know the feel of her hands. To wonder whether she'd ever wondered about another woman the way Bertrice did.

"I suppose it is good," Miss Beauchamps said. "I have it so often, I rarely think of it. If I had your money, I would…" But she trailed off and didn't finish.

"You would?"

"I can't choose," Miss Beauchamps said after a while. "There's too much. Sweets, I think."

A little silence fell. Another bite of that marvelous cheese toast; Bertrice chanced another look at the woman who sat across from her.

When Bertrice had been young and foolish, she'd thought beauty was as simple as clear, smooth skin, wide eyes, willowy silhouettes…the usual, really.

Decades of watching beauty had changed her. What was meant by "beauty" altered over the years—

fashion demanded first plump, then slender. One year, brunettes were all the rage; the next, it was blonde hair. The noses that society raved over went from small to Grecian to snub.

Nobody would call Miss Beauchamps beautiful, she didn't think; even decades younger, had she been on the marriage mart, men known for sharp wits and sharper tongues would undoubtedly have amused crowds by mocking her.

Miss Beauchamps no doubt knew that. She probably knew in excruciating detail precisely what fun men might have at her expense.

Still, she drew the eye in a way that Bertrice could not explain, and did not want to attempt to understand. Her cheeks were round and ruddy, like a teakettle on the hearth. She sat stiff-backed, feet on the floor, but there was something about the way she looked at the wall that made Bertrice think she was seeing some country far beyond England.

She wanted to know what she was looking at. It wasn't just attraction. It was a pull within her, beckoning her closer.

"It must be nice," Miss Beauchamps said, "to not have to worry about money."

Bertrice worried about money; she worried a great deal about how she would leave it. But that wasn't what Miss Beauchamps meant.

"I suppose it is," she said slowly. "I rarely think of it."

Miss Beauchamps sighed and stood, slicing an apple before handing Bertrice two quarters. "Why did your doctor think you need a restorative treatment, then? If it's not too impolite to ask."

"Oh, I had fallen into a bit of a rut." She looked upward. "I didn't want to do anything. Nothing tasted good anymore. That sort of thing."

"Was there a reason?"

There was always a reason. Bertrice sat and breathed through the pain of hers for a moment before answering. "Well. Mrs. Lakeland passed away two years ago. Then Mrs. Nightwood. Then Mrs. Trouridge. There, just like that, in the space of nineteen months." Her voice did not tremble, not in the slightest. "My entire card group gone." Especially Ellie Nightwood, Ellie who had brought her through the worst of her marriage and saved her heart. "Everyone kept telling me to cheer up because I was lucky to still be alive and hale and hearty."

Miss Beauchamps made a sympathetic noise.

"I *am* lucky to be alive," Bertrice said, shaking off her shoulders as if she could shrug off that cloying sympathy. "I *am*. I don't want to be dead."

"Being alive doesn't spare you from grief. Rather the reverse."

She could feel a lump of emotion welling up in her, and Bertrice hated lumps of emotion. "It's hard to lose friends. And at this age…" No, there it was— stupid emotion again. She gritted her teeth and waited for it to pass.

"At this age," Miss Beauchamps finished for her, "everyone looks through you as if you're not even there."

"*Yes.*" Bertrice shut her eyes. "Precisely." That solid mass of emotion persisted, still damnably present. "So you know how it is."

Miss Beauchamps shrugged one shoulder. "I am what the papers call a surplus woman. There are so many of us—women who have never married, who make their own way in society—that we aren't even people any longer. We're just statistics to be presented. The most I can hope is that I'll be pointed to as a warning to young women, to secure their men before they turn into me. I wasn't alone most of the time. But my dearest friend went with her sister to Boston six years ago. Since then, I've been like this." She gestured around her. "Save for letters."

"Yes." Bertrice swallowed. "It's not the same for widows, but…it is. I had…" It was hard to talk about her friends still; her throat tightened with emotion. "My friends aren't here any longer, and now that they're gone I want to scream that I'm real, I'm still a person. I don't stop existing because I can no longer have children. There was no point in my life where I ceased having dreams for the future. There was no time when I stopped wanting friends and camaraderie and—"

She cut herself off.

Miss Beauchamps looked at her. "And?"

For one beat, Bertrice considered not saying a thing. But she'd learned long ago that there was no point in being circumspect. Her heart was wrapped in suffocating folds of cloth, each layer a regret made of things she'd never said. There was no point holding back. "Sexual attraction at my age is the worst," she admitted. "Everyone acts as if one should naturally outgrow all wants."

She still felt it beneath her skin—the desire to touch and be touched, to hold and be held. To be affirmed in the present. To be important to someone else. She'd once been thought beautiful—that had passed with her youth—but she still longed to be thought pretty. Just because she had grown old, just because she'd ceased to match the fresh-faced standard of loveliness, didn't mean that she'd lost her want.

People spoke of desire as if it were the province of the young. But here was Bertrice at seventy-three, still yearning.

"But you don't seem to like men," Miss Beauchamps offered slowly. "At all. Do you mean…?"

Again, Bertrice was past the point of dissembling. "If God intended women to only have relations with men, then why did He give women fingers and tongues?"

Miss Beauchamps tilted her head to look at her. She didn't often do it. Her eyes crossed just a little, giving the expression a hint of sweetness. Sweet, and for a second, Bertrice wanted to taste. She wanted to know more about the lines on her brow, the tips of her fingers. She wanted to lean in and—

Miss Beauchamps flushed and quickly dropped her gaze to her tea cup.

Just as well. Bertrice didn't need to do anything hasty. "Sometimes, I dream of finding a young thing of forty."

The tea cup slammed on the saucer. Bertrice looked up to see the other woman standing abruptly. She piled the empty dishes atop each other—loudly, angrily—and marched to a basin on the other side of the room.

Oh. *Oh.*

Bertrice watched as Miss Beauchamps violently wiped down the plates, then wiped the table where she'd cut the bread and cheese with a damp cloth. She went to the window, finally, opened it, and poured the gray water into the street below. A blast of cold air rushed in before she could close it once more.

"Miss Beauchamps," Bertrice started, "I didn't mean—"

"Never mind. It's nothing."

"That's just false. It is clearly *something.* When I said—"

"It's nothing," Miss Beauchamps repeated, securing the windows once again and setting the basin back in place. Belatedly, Bertrice realized that the woman had done all the labor that evening—the preparing, the toasting, the cleaning—and that there were no servants.

Oh. How rude. She hadn't thought. She hadn't helped. How… How utterly manlike of her. A flicker of shame went through her.

"It's nothing," Miss Beauchamps said a third time. "Just this—you want a forty-year old, and I'm standing right *here*. I told you how I felt, but even *you* don't see me as anything except surplus."

Oh. There it was, a second flicker of shame, this one deeper.

That's bad, Bertrice. Doubly bad, because it was true.

Miss Beauchamps just exhaled and shut her eyes. The anger in her pose tensed into stiff propriety once again. "Oh, dear." She turned away. "How very awkward of me. I shouldn't have—that is, I didn't mean to imply…" She trailed off. "Never mind it all. We should get ready for bed."

Bertrice hadn't really let herself think about bed. The single bed was large enough for two—maybe. Plenty of room if they didn't mind limbs touching. Scarcely enough, if they laid on their sides at the opposite edge of the mattress.

Miss Beauchamp's gowns seemed easier to undo than Bertrice's. It had been ages since she had undone her own gowns, and she didn't want to ask for help, especially now that she'd made such an ass of herself. She tried her best to undo the buttons up her back, but her arms didn't quite reach and her fingers cramped—

"Here," Miss Beauchamps said brusquely, and Bertrice shut her eyes at the dance of fingertips down her back. It was business-like, quick and impartial.

No, you don't understand, she imagined herself saying. *I like you just fine.* It wouldn't make the situation less awkward.

"Thank you," she said, but Miss Beauchamps did not answer.

They washed in silence.

She needed to offer something like an apology. She knew it. When the pitcher ran low, she made sure to fill it from the bucket. She hashed through the muddle of her thoughts.

It wasn't until they'd gotten stiffly into bed— curling on opposite sides as far from each other as they could get, and yet so close that one wrong move, and they'd touch—that Bertrice spoke.

"What I meant." She swallowed. "I meant that I wanted someone who would be sure to outlive me. I don't want to suffer through another loss. The last one who left…" She couldn't find words. She could feel that dark malaise that had taken over her. She'd been adrift in grief. "It was too much. The one thing that having money allows is that I *could*, I suppose. Find a forty-year-old."

Miss Beauchamps did not respond, not for a long while. Her breath was even in the cold of the night— even, but not slow enough for sleep. Bertrice bit her lip. She was *not* a man, she wasn't. She wasn't going to demand forgiveness when she'd been the one in the wrong. She stared blankly into the dark.

"It still sounds to me as if you mean that someone like me hasn't anything to give you," Miss Beauchamps said.

It did, it did, but…

"And," Miss Beauchamps continued, "it sounds to me as if you're afraid you've nothing to offer but your money."

Bertrice breathed in that hurt. It was true—all too

true. She knew how people talked of women like her —as if she were empty, all worth leached from her by the passing of time. Even her doctor, less terrible than most men, had thought of her as nothing but her funds.

She wasn't, though. She was real. She was still here, alive and dreaming.

"My dearest friend died two years ago." Bertrice hugged her arms to her chest. Friend wasn't a close enough word for what she had been. Lover wasn't a close enough word. What did you call the person who made your life worth living? What did you call her, when you weren't supposed to even have her at all? "I *am* lonely and I'm sad and I'm so, so scared. People tell me that I am supposed to mellow with age, but I care as fiercely as ever. And caring hurts. I'm frightened of caring."

Miss Beauchamps sighed.

"You're not surplus," Bertrice said. "No woman has ever needed a man to be enough."

"Tell the rest of the world." Miss Beauchamps turned in bed. "I don't dare stick my neck out, not once. If I had money, I'd…"

Once again, she paused. Once again, Bertrice asked. "What would you do?"

"I'd stop worrying," Miss Beauchamps breathed.

Maybe that was when Bertrice realized what she needed to do. Not much; just ease the burdens that made Miss Beauchamps's shoulders so tense. *Show* her that she wasn't surplus, because telling wasn't enough. Maybe confess the incoherent thoughts she'd had over dinner.

She could feel the other woman turning in the bed, and with it came the awareness that they were close physically, and not in any other way.

Start slow, Bertrice. You've hurt her, and you have questions to ask of your solicitor. Start slow.

She wasn't good at slow, but she tried. "Do you think you might show me how to use the…the cheese toasty thing? Tomorrow evening?"

A huff. "Yes," Miss Beauchamps muttered. "I suppose I could."

"I'm sorry I did so little to help with dinner tonight," Bertrice tried again.

"Your knee looked as if it pained you. I didn't mind. Truly."

The silence stretched longer. "By the way," Bertrice heard herself asking, "what do you suppose would be the most annoying way to wake up?"

One last huff. "Dear heavens. Do I want to know why you're asking me that? Or am I better off living in ignorance?"

Bertrice smiled in the dark. "Yes, I rather think you want to know why I'm asking. You'll like it. We're going to have fun."

~

The sun had been two hours up. The streets were crowded. Violetta herself had never been the sort to lie abed letting daylight waste in any event; she would have personally called the hour closer to noon than morning. Nobody could have thought it *early*. Nobody rational, that was.

But then, they were talking about Mr. Robert Cappish. Rational had no place in the life of a man such as he. They stood just outside his door in the rooming house. They had waited until the last man other than Cappish had vacated the premises. Cappish was still in his rooms, no doubt sleeping the sleep of a man who had no idea what was in store for him.

"Here," Mrs. Martin whispered, as they got into position just outside his door. "You should have this."

A touch of her hand, skin against skin, and Violetta felt herself blush, remembering what she'd admitted last night. She had essentially implied that she found Mrs. Martin attractive, and *that* had been an embarrassment and a half. But Mrs. Martin was just giving her the stick, a firm wand of oak, as thick as her little finger, and twelve inches long.

"But—" Her protest was a whisper; why, she didn't know, when the entire point of this exercise was to be loud. "But I haven't the faintest idea how to—"

Mrs. Martin's eyes twinkled in her face. "That's the point. You don't need to *know*. Just do it."

It felt utterly ridiculous to turn to the small group that had gathered in the hall. Three men, two women. Violetta had met them years ago when they had gone caroling for charity. They had been the most successful charity carolers she had ever encountered, mostly because everyone they encountered emptied their pockets in a tremendous rush to hurry them on.

"On three," Mrs. Martin said. "One, two—"

Violetta knew nothing of conducting. She didn't know the music. She had no idea what she was doing. But there was no escaping the force of Mrs. Martin's personality. She raised the stick.

"Three!"

Down went Violetta's hand.

"Hallelujah," bellowed the chorus—off-key, out of synchrony, and extremely loud. *"Hallelujah."*

Beside her, Mrs. Martin begin laughing.

It was utterly ridiculous. Violetta had spent all her

life trying to fit in, trying to be unobtrusive. And yet at the first sound of those notes, something inside her seemed to wake up—as if the out-of-tune song blew air over the embers of her anger.

Stupid Robert Cappish, stupid, *stupid* Robert Cappish. Stupid Mr. Toggert, stupid men everywhere who thought she was nothing, and stupid *her* for agreeing. For *letting* them think so.

She waved her arms wildly in what she hoped was the universal signal for *more noise, now, please.*

"HALLELUJAH, HALLELUJAH, *HALLELUJAH.*"

She would have bet anything that the chorus had no sense of music at all, but they responded to her gesticulations with wild enthusiasm, redoubling their volume.

"FOR THE LORD GOD OMNIPOTENT REIGNITH!"

A little doopsy-doo with her conducting stick— what on earth was the thing even called?—and they followed her cue, tilting even more off key.

Her face almost felt as if it would crack from the smile that grew.

Maybe Mr. Cappish was waking up. Maybe he was banging on the door. Maybe he was shouting for them to be quiet, but it wouldn't matter. They couldn't hear his protests. The cacophony was deafening; the man bellowing in the back had brought along cymbals, which he crashed together not at all in time to the music. It was the most glorious dissonance, and it went on and on.

"AND HE SHALL REIGN FOR EVER AND EVER."

Out of the corner of her eye, she saw the door behind her open; she turned quickly.

Mr. Cappish stood red-eyed and angry in front of them. He must have dressed hastily. The tails of his shirt were untucked; his jacket was twisted at the collar. His mouth moved. He was undoubtedly saying words. She couldn't hear a single one.

Violetta felt a wild surge of delight. He was talking to her, and she was drowning him out. For the first time in her life, *she* was drowning out someone *else.* She turned back to the choir and frantically waved her arms.

"KING OF KINGS!" they bellowed. "LORD OF LORDS!"

He stomped to stand in front of her, waving his arms, and—well—she supposed they *would* have to deliver their message eventually. Violetta sighed and let her arms drop.

The choir lapsed into silence raggedly, person by person.

"How dare you!" He glared at her. "Sleep is *important* to restore one's mind and health. To interrupt it in this manner is—it's really just entirely uncalled for, Miss Beauchamps. How *dare* you!"

"Robby Bobkins," said Mrs. Martin behind her, "if you have something to say, you should say it to my face."

It was interesting to watch his face turn white. First, the blood drained from his nose—impressive, considering how red it had been. Then from his lips. Then his forehead went pale, then his cheeks turned waxy. He turned around, looking almost green.

"Aunt…Aunt Bertrice." He plastered a fake smile on his face.

"Robby Bobkins, I *told* you I was going to make your life miserable. When have I ever not meant what I said?"

"Ah… But, Aunt Bertrice." He shut his eyes. "First things first. I must please, once again, ask you to not refer to me as…that name."

"Which name? Robby Bobkins?" Mrs. Martin spoke half as loud as the chorus had been singing—which was very loud indeed.

"Mr. Cappish, please. Or, as I said, you may call me 'Cappy.' I ask for only this small form of civility. I'm sure if we could just talk matters out, we could come to an understanding."

Mrs. Martin looked at him for a long moment, before nodding. "Yes, I think we can. Let us compromise. From here on out, I will call you 'Mr. Cappish, a despicable bag of diseased meat.'"

The Terrible Nephew blinked.

"Ladies and gentlemen of the choir, this is Mr. Cappish, a despicable bag of diseased meat." She looked at her nephew expectantly. "There, I've shown that I'm capable of compromise. Now will you promise not to rape women, or do you need an additional title?"

"I—Aunt Bertrice, that's—" He sputtered. "That's not any better than Robby Bobkins!"

"Men." Aunt Bertrice shook her head. "Never satisfied, no matter how hard you try to please 'em. Well, I tried. Miss Beauchamps, if you will do the honors?"

Violetta bit her lip, and then leaned into the choir, whispering her orders. They listened carefully.

"FOR BEHOLD," they began singing, "DARKNESS SHALL COVER THE EARTH."

Robby Bobkins groaned and retreated into his room.

Ten minutes later, he came out, freshly shaven and somewhat cleaned up. His ruffled collar betrayed his haste, however; he pushed past the throng at his doorstep, stumbling to the stairs and brushing lint off his coat as he went.

Violetta stopped her choir—when had she started

thinking of them as *her* choir?—and let Mrs. Martin give instructions.

"We will be following him," she said. "Let's pick some good pieces?"

"I have an idea," Violetta heard herself say.

And so it was that they caught up with him three minutes later as he was strolling down the street, tipping his hat in a friendly fashion. He didn't see them coming behind him. He didn't even suspect it.

He had no idea what was about to happen, not even as Violetta raised her conducting-stick-thingy and waved it in the air.

"ROBBY BOBKINS!" the choir sang to the tune of the Hallelujah Chorus. "ROBBY BOBKINS! ROBBY BOBKINS, ROBBY BOBKINS, ROBBY BOBKINS!"

He broke into a run, and something stiff in Violetta's chest melted at that.

It was worth it. Whatever happened—whether Violetta got her money, or if she was exposed as a fraud and tossed in prison—it didn't matter. It was worth it to see him scamper off like a frightened rabbit. She and her ragged choir did their best to follow him—it didn't help the quality of the music any, but it could hardly hurt—all the way through "FRIEND OF FRIENDS!"

They followed until Mrs. Martin was lagging far behind. Violetta stopped two streets down, gestured the choir into silence, and waited for Mrs. Martin to catch up.

"He'll be angry about that," Mrs. Martin remarked. There was a small smile on her face.

"I know." Violetta tried to remember that she was in public. She straightened her shoulders and shoved that ridiculous desire to laugh deep inside her. "Isn't it glorious?"

CHAPTER FOUR

The sun was high and bright overhead. The chorus had been paid, and Bertrice had decided on the next entertainment for the day.

It was not quite two in the afternoon—the time when Bertrice usually found herself retreating to her room for a nap for want of something else to do. She'd spent months staring up at the canopy of her too-large bed, hoping for some surcease from her daily boredom.

Now, she sat in Hyde Park on a bench. They'd wandered here over several miles—mostly by hired cabs, stopping here and there to duck into shops. Bertrice's hips ached—a good ache, the sort of ache she'd not felt in years. Her knee...well, that was less of a good ache.

Lord, Bertrice sometimes forgot she wasn't forty any longer. She surreptitiously rubbed the joint. She'd need to find a cabriolet to take them straight back, no questions asked, *that* was for certain.

They'd sunk onto this bench, trees and grass and the distant glitter of silver waters all around them. She and Miss Beauchamps had procured jacket potatoes from an establishment at the edge of the park, cooked to perfection and slathered in butter and salt. They'd purchased bottles of soda water. They sat close to each other, wielding forks that Miss Beauchamps had produced from a pocket as if she were some sort of magician.

The first bite of potato was meltingly perfect. For so long, sustenance had felt like dust. She'd had no interest, no excitement. It had seemed a miracle last night to enjoy one meal; it seemed impossible that she could enjoy two. And yet here she was.

There was nothing she could point to that made this potato exceptionally good. Maybe it was the salt. Maybe it was the sun.

Maybe it was the way that Violetta Beauchamps sat next to her, ankles crossed demurely, potato in wax paper held in front of her.

She'd heard it said that hunger was the best sauce, but company was a seasoning that had been in short supply over the last years. Maybe that was it.

"I haven't had this much fun in ages," Miss Beauchamps said.

"Neither have I." She looked over at the other woman and felt an ache in her chest, the remnants of grief still lodged in her ribcage.

"All my life," Miss Beauchamps said, "I've done everything *right.* I was a demure little girl for my parents. I took care of them. I was introduced to men, and when nothing came of that, I…" She paused, her mouth temporarily thinning, then looked up with a sigh. "I…inherited the rooming house. And still I did precisely what I was supposed to do. I kept complete, fair records. I rented rooms to men of good families. I was polite and kind, even when my tenants were in arrears, even when they threatened me. I was always, always kind. I thought if I was, they'd have to be kind back. Eventually."

Bertrice sighed. "It was different for me. People *had* to be civil to me; I'm rich."

"Did they, though?"

She thought about the way her nephew talked to her—as if he always knew better, as if her eyes and her heart were suspect, as if she should be willing to substitute whatever facts suited him in place of what she knew to be true.

"It's a peculiar sort of civility. I must be humored. But they don't actually listen to me. Even if their words are polite."

Miss Beauchamps took another bite of potato. Her tongue flicked out to meet her fork, and for a second Bertrice felt as if her entire being was caught on that motion, so prosaic and yet so striking. Oh, to be a chunk of potato. Miss Beauchamps chewed and swallowed; it felt almost sinful to watch. She looked up to meet Bertrice's gaze, and, for a moment, paused, mouth open a fraction, before flushing and looking away.

"Tell me, Mrs. Martin. Do you often engage choruses to bebother men who have fallen from your graces?"

Mrs. Martin. It was polite, yes, but it felt so...so wrong. So *distancing*. Mrs. Martin was the label society applied to the wife of her husband, and that rat-fiend was long and thankfully dead.

"Bertrice," she said.

There was a pause. Miss Beauchamps frowned at her as if she did not know what she meant.

"My given name," she clarified. "It's Bertrice."

"I know? We signed a contract, did we not?"

"Well, use it," Bertrice told her. "Nobody has since my...dear friend passed away. It feels like it's getting rusty."

"And you expect me to polish it off for you?"

Bertrice felt herself flush. She hadn't meant to imply that she wanted the woman to act as if she were in service. But who did she talk to but servants at all any longer? "I didn't mean—that is, oh, *damn* it all—"

Miss Beauchamps's eyes flashed bright. "I was teasing. I can't call you Bertrice if I can't tease you, you know."

Oh. *Oh.* Miss Beauchamps bumped her shoulder, lightly, and Bertrice felt an irrepressible smile rise to her face. "Is that so?"

"It's so. I tease my friends, just a little." She looked over her shoulder, briefly. "I did before Lily went overseas, at least."

"Well." Bertrice looked over. *Teasing.* God, it hadn't been so long ago that she and her friends had all been alive. *They'd* teased her. They'd also sat with her during the worst of her marriage, finding excuses to get her out of London when he was in the city and reasons to bring her *into* London when he was rusticating. And she'd done her best by them, too.

Her friends had been an extension of her heart.

If Ellie had been here, she would have teased her, too—telling her to stop worrying, reminding her that she was alive.

Bright sunshine was spilling onto the crown of Bertrice's head. It felt like it was sinking into her being, lighting her to the tips of her toes. "That's...nice. That's very nice."

"My name is Violetta," said Miss Beauchamps. "And you haven't answered my question, you know. Do you often bebother men who fall from your good graces?"

Bertrice thought about the look on her Terrible Nephew's face. "Not often enough."

"It's awfully rude of us. I feel as if we shouldn't

enjoy it."

"As rude as not paying rent for two years?"

Miss Beauchamps—no, Violetta—pursed her lips.

"They don't listen," Bertrice said. "And he doesn't listen to *you* differently than he doesn't listen to me— but he's still not listening. Following him around with a chorus has been the only thing that's received a response so far. Let's keep it up, shall we?"

The woman had—technically—signed a contract agreeing to do so, but nothing in the contract mentioned terrible carolers or farm animals or any of the other awful, vengeful ideas that Bertrice had been nursing in anger.

She held her breath as Violetta seemed to consider this.

"You know," Bertrice offered, "if you'd like, we could do it the easy way. Go to the constables; have him tossed out for failure to pay. But I tried purchasing his debts and having him tossed in debtor's prison. It didn't work."

That had been back in the days when rage was all Bertrice had. She had already felt empty and grief-stricken; rage had been welcome, as *some* sort of emotion rather than an absolute void of nothing. It had burned through her like a fire. She'd felt like she could have set the world ablaze. But she'd been contained in stone, doomed to burn and smolder impotently.

"What happened?"

"They found out I was his aunt and insisted it was a family matter, nothing for the courts." Bertrice sighed. She'd felt like cold ash for so long. No appetite. No longing. No hope, just the smothered embers of her resentment.

And yet here Violetta was, sitting beside her. Violetta's hand rested on her own knee; her knee was so close that if Bertrice leaned in even the slightest amount, their knuckles would bump.

"Ah," Violetta said softly. "Of course."

"I've screamed on the inside, too," Bertrice confessed. "I've screamed on the outside. I've screamed until I thought there was nothing left of me but my voice, and then I lost my voice. And still I kept screaming."

Violetta's eyes lifted to hers. It was just a glance—she seemed shy of the connection—but the dark glow in her eyes felt like a touch. Smoldering ember to ember, voice to voice, scream to scream. Then her head dipped down once more. "I never screamed aloud, and yet I lost my voice from disuse."

Bertrice let her hand drift to her right, a knuckle's width, enough to brush against the other woman ever so slightly. Ember to ember, spark to spark. She could feel it building inside her—as if the act of hearing and listening, repeated over and over, could make a furnace of her.

"It is up to the two of us, then," Violetta said. "Two is more than one."

One was impossible. One was contained. Alone, Mrs. Martin had felt cribbed in, made of complaints and unable to move. Two was a more dangerous number.

And then Violetta clinched it. She looked over at Mrs. Martin, and she asked the most wonderful question. "Well, then. What will we do to him next?"

～

"Good Lord." The lodger stopped at the head of the rooming house stairwell, frowning at the procession that Violetta and Bertrice were heading. "What on earth are you intending to do with these animals?"

Drat. Violetta turned to him and put on her most placating face. They had made it up to the first floor, to within feet of Mr. Cappish's door, before being stopped, and she hardly wanted to give an explanation.

You see, Mr. Lornville, she imagined herself saying, *we are attempting to bedevil a horrible man.*

They'd come up with the idea together. Bertrice had sent a message by courier to her man-of-affairs. What the fellow had to do with farm animals, Violetta didn't know, but in short order, some poor clerk had procured a procession of women with geese in cages. The geese girls were currently carting their goods to the top of the stairs, while the birds hissed unhappily through the wooden bars. A few feathers marked their passage up to the first floor.

But Mr. Lornville was frowning at them. He was in his fifties—a barrister, although he scarcely practiced law—and very sure of his own significance.

To be fair, one didn't need to be particularly haughty to object to geese in one's rooming house.

"We're taking them up these stairs," Bertrice said. "Quite obviously. Have you no sense?"

Mr. Lornville's eyes narrowed. "I live up here." He peered into the nearest cage, and was rewarded with the responding hiss of the devil bird inside. "What do you intend to do with these geese in this rooming house?"

"Release them," Bertrice snapped impatiently. "Don't worry; they won't be in your quarters."

"They're loud," the man countered, "and geese are filthy, violent animals. They don't belong in *any* sort of house, let alone a rooming house. On whose orders is this being done?"

Bertrice gestured nonchalantly. "Miss Beauchamps approved it."

Violetta swallowed around a lump of fear in her throat.

It had only been three days since she had been sacked, and Mr. Toggert had obviously not informed the tenants of her displacement. But for a few scant hours, Violetta had been so immersed in their plans that she had forgotten the truth. She was not the owner of the rooming house. Mr. Lornville knew that, and he could expose her lies right now.

Mr. Lornville made an unhappy noise. "You can't do this, Miss Beauchamps. I don't know which tenant asked for such a ridiculous thing, but *I* don't approve, and I also live here. I would like to file a formal complaint."

"Oh," Violetta said through her fear. "Well."

What would Bertrice do? She wouldn't stand in place, rooted in fear. Bertrice, indeed, had not let so much as an eyelash flicker out of place during this entire exchange. Her arms were folded aggressively, cane dangling from one hand as if to suggest she could beat the man with it as easily as use it to assist her ascent of the staircase.

What would Bertrice say? She would—ah. There. Violetta drew herself up straight and made what she hoped was a gracious movement with her right hand. "Your formal complaint has been noted."

"Noted?" Mr. Lornville frowned. "Just noted? Have you not considered my request beyond that one second? I say, Miss Beauchamps."

"It's been noted," Violetta repeated. "The geese are allowed." Then, from some well of unknown creativity, she added, "We have agreed to conduct an experiment on living with fowl in London. Food practices which relegate the production of eggs and meat to far-flung farms may result in contamination during transport. We have therefore—"

Luckily, Mr. Lornville interrupted her before she had to provide any further explanation for this ridiculous flight of fancy. "I say. I don't wish to live on a farm. It can't be hygienic."

"The geese *are* trained," Bertrice lied next to her.

"Lots of people live on farms," Violetta added. "Many of them don't die, I've heard." Technically, they all probably died at some point. She amended her answer. "At least not out of turn." She hoped that was the case. She'd never been anywhere near a farm in her life.

"This is simply unacceptable. Listen to the noise! *Smell* them! If I have to, I will take this complaint—"

"To the authorities?" Violetta interrupted, before the man could go and ruin everything by mentioning Mr. Toggert, the man who had sacked her. She had a brief vision in her mind of how he would take this. Mr. Toggert, and his calm complacency. Mr. Toggert, and the look in his eye as he'd told her she had let profits fallen. Mr. Toggert, waving off the comment that he'd been the one at fault, waving off her proof, her entire life. It had been a pretense to avoid paying her pension—and he'd lied to her and held her to blame when she was the one who'd warned him in the first place.

Damn Mr. Toggert. Damn him to hell.

Better yet, damn him to unprofitability.

"Of course," she heard herself saying before she could think through the consequences, "I will release you from your lease. Due to changed circumstances and the like."

Bertrice looked at her in surprise.

Violetta had no authority to do anything of the sort. This was not the sort of lie she should tell—she knew it, the moment it came off her lips. But if Mr. Toggert lost all his tenants because he hadn't taken the necessary steps to replace her...whose fault was that, really?

Yours, actually, some portion of her mind that insisted on the truth whispered. *It's your fault.*

"I will give you two pounds," Bertrice said, "if you'll sign papers agreeing to quit the premises within three days."

Mr. Lornville blinked. So did Violetta.

"Well, he does have a valid lease," Bertrice pointed out, "and I do believe the experiments would be easier, if we had fewer people here. If you wish not to be part of it—by all means, we would be delighted to help you leave."

"Well." Mr. Lornville tilted his head. "Perhaps... I'll have to move all my things, you know."

"Four pounds," Mrs. Martin said with a shrug, and Violetta refused to let herself feel anything more than a hint of jealousy at being able to throw around such a monstrous sum without blinking an eye.

"Five?"

"Only because these experiments are very important," Bertrice said solemnly.

Mr. Lornville smiled brilliantly and extended a hand. "That's very good of you. Very good indeed."

Bertrice did not shake his hand. Instead, she wrote out a draft on her bank, and had him sign a paper, before sending him on his way. The geese hissed angrily at him as he passed.

"Well?" Bertrice turned to Violetta. "What are you waiting for?"

Violetta took out the master key, which she had failed to return to Mr. Toggert, and unlocked the door to Mr. Cappish's room. He'd not emerged at all during the entire conversation—but it was nine in

the morning, and a handful of geese and a bit of dis-
cussion were hardly enough to wake a man who re-
quired a deafening chorus to rouse him from
slumber at that hour.

They gestured silently for the geese girls to enter;
she could hear the *snick* as the cages opened. The
women dashed back into the hall in a rush.

That was it. They'd loosed nine geese in the Terrible Nephew's room.

Violetta shut the door behind them. She locked it,
for good measure.

"One," Bertrice counted. "Two. Three. Fo—"

"What in the blazing devil's hell is going on!" they
heard Mr. Cappish shout from inside the room.

Bertrice dissolved into laughter.

And oh, Violetta should be scared. She was offi-
cially doing things that she had no business doing.
She was now violating the law in new and interesting
ways, and she should be too scared to do anything
except cower.

But laughter was contagious, too, and she found
herself cackling aloud as Mr. Cappish swore up a
storm.

When they'd laughed so hard her sides ached, she
turned to Bertrice.

"What would you like to do today?" she asked.

It was almost like being on holiday—a holiday
where she lived in her own rooms and tormented
men for fun and profit.

"Maybe see the Houses of Parliament?" Bertrice
commented. "I never have before."

"Are you sure? They're full of men, you know."

"I know," Bertrice said glumly. "What's worse,
they burned down decades ago, and I wasn't even
there to see it. But we can have fun imagining what it
was like, can't we?"

CHAPTER FIVE

Violetta managed to hold in her emotions for another handful of days.

Honestly, she hadn't realized she was holding anything. Or maybe she'd been holding on to so much for so long that hiding her pain felt normal.

In the end, a tree outside Westminster Abbey set her off.

The sun was out, and a few days of damp cold had given way to a bout of unseasonable sunshine. Perfect, Bertrice had said, for a little tour of London sights.

Violetta had agreed because Bertrice was something like an avalanche—there was no point trying to stop her. Besides, Violetta had discovered that there was a great deal of joy to be had when those rocks fell on other people.

It gave Violetta a tiny taste of what it might have been like, if her life had taken an upward turn instead of sliding down. If she'd had money. If her income had been just a twitch higher. If her parents had retained anything to pass on to her.

Bertrice had sent a note off to some man-of-affairs somewhere, and they'd been given a tour of the

Abbey. After, a servant had blankets and a picnic lunch waiting for them. The man had stood under a tree—an old, gnarled oak with spreading branches—just to hold them a prime spot. The tree had dropped most of its leaves for the winter, and sunshine flickered through the branches.

It had *definitely* been the tree that had set Violetta off.

Certainly not Bertrice setting her hand on one rippling root, looking up through the branches at the blue sky overhead. She'd said absolutely nothing of import. Just this: "What a marvelous, beautiful tree this is!"

It *was* a marvelous tree, shaped by time and gardeners into twisted, labyrinthine splendor.

And yet that one remark stole the air from Violetta's lungs. She'd felt as if she were punched in the gut, as if all those years of grasping and holding everything in place were suddenly too much.

"Why?" Violetta had heard herself ask, her tone just a touch querulous.

Bertrice turned to her. "You don't agree?"

Violetta didn't know what to think. She hardly knew what she felt. "I just want to know *why* you think it."

"Well." Bertrice looked at the tree, frowning. "There's the bark, to start. Don't you think bark on old trees is picturesque? It's got—oh, I don't know the proper terms. But it's split. It's got ravines, you know. Proper texture. None of that smooth, boring stuff that young trees boast."

Something dark and sharp took form in Violetta's breast. "Go on." It came out on a hiss.

Bertrice looked bewildered. "Well...then...the shape. Look at that branch there, the way it dips and then rises. Or there, where those two branches have been rubbing together. Or *there*—there's a story about the left half of this tree, don't you think? I can almost imagine the gale that stripped away all but the heaviest branches, and they're only now growing back, a thicket of little twigs on a giant oak like this."

Violetta looked at the branches overhead, her teeth gritted, trying not to let her eyes water. Trying not to feel, just as she'd spent decades not letting herself respond to every last insult that she had been supposed to take as her due.

"All nature is like that, really," Bertrice had continued. "A boring straight stream is nothing compared to a rivulet that has carved its path deep into the forest, rock worn away, banks covered in moss. The human eye is drawn to difference."

The tight knot of hurt that Violetta had been nursing all her life flared. It flared into anger and self-pity and dismay. Then—like a wildfire set on a dry meadow—it raced past those simpler emotions directly into confounding rage.

"No doubt," she snapped. "Trees and streams and valleys and beaches alike. All of them grow more beautiful with age. Even men in their own way receive more respect. But it's not *all* of nature. It's all of nature except human women."

Bertrice turned to her, eyes wide.

"It's not me," Violetta snapped. "Nobody praises the texture of my skin, now that I'm no longer smooth as a sapling. Over the years, I've grown rounder and more lumpy, but when it's a human being with cares and feelings instead of a tree, *I'm* considered *disgusting.*"

"Violetta," Bertrice murmured. She tentatively reached out a hand. "*I* don't consider you disgusting."

"Even though I'm not a sprightly young thing of forty? How good of you. Even if it were true, you're one out of—how many people are there on this planet? Millions? Ha." She plucked morosely at the blanket beneath her. "But it's not just age. I've *never* been beautiful. My eyes cross, no matter how hard I try. My hands are so ugly that store clerks wince when I count change. Why is it that everyone can find a bloody *tree* more beautiful than a human woman who shares the same properties?"

She was raising her voice. A woman—much younger—gave her a disapproving glare and a sniff.

Violetta had never used the word *bloody* in her life. She hadn't even realized it was in her vocabulary.

She shut her eyes and felt her anger mingle with shame. She reached out, trying to catch hold of her unruly emotions. "I apologize for shouting. It's not *your* fault. It's been like this forever, and every time I think I'm at the bottom of humanity's care, I descend one rung further and discover how wrong I was. There's always another rung."

"There shouldn't be a bottom." Bertrice's hand was still stretched out, not quite reaching Violetta. Her fingers twitched forward, then stopped abruptly. "There shouldn't be a ladder."

Maybe she pulled back just now because she thought Violetta untouchably ugly. Maybe it was because they weren't the touching sort of friends. Whatever the reason, that hurt too.

Violetta felt little stinging beads of moisture form at the corner of her eyes, and let out a noise of frustration. Anger, and now this? Crying was for fools.

"Violetta."

She sniffed, refusing to look.

"You're right. It's not fair."

She shook her head. "My mother always told me it was what was inside that really counted, but I realized quickly it was a lie. They never say such things to pretty women."

"They don't," Bertrice whispered.

And Bertrice would know. Age had been kinder to her. Her locks were white and easy to pin in place, unlike Violetta's unruly mass of salt-and-pepper. Her hair had always been thick and curly; age had made her gray hairs coarser and downright untamable. Bertrice's features were pleasant and symmetric; she was slim enough that she had little to sag. She had wealth and beauty and the ability to command, and what did Violetta have?

Lies and a bank account that would deplete itself before she did everyone the favor of passing away.

She swiped away the moisture on her cheeks.

Bertrice's fingers once again twitched, then moved to lie still on her knee. "It's lies," she said. "They lie to us all. And sometimes we're idiots and we believe them, even if we know better."

"Yes."

"They lie to us, but we needn't lie to each other." She looked over to Violetta, looking *at* her, not through her. Her gaze touched her hands, then traveled up her arms. She took in every part that Violetta had ever been told was ugly.

"Don't you think?" Bertrice asked.

Yes, Violetta almost said. It nearly came out as a plea. And then she remembered the rooming house— the one she didn't own. She remembered the contract and the lie. She'd waited years and years, hoping someone would see the inner beauty her mother had told her was all that mattered. Sixty-nine years she'd waited. Sixty-nine years, until she'd given up. Because destiny was cruel, it had delivered that someone the very instant that she had capitulated.

Violetta closed her eyes.

Her fingers twitched of their own accord, moving toward the point where Bertrice's hand rested on her knee. So close she could almost feel the contact.

"I want it," she confessed to the tree and Bertrice. "I want honesty more than anything. But I don't believe it's possible anymore."

"You know what I see when I look at this oak?"

Violetta shook her head.

"Centuries have passed, and it's still here."

It survived. That was it—that was all Violetta could hope for, all she could ever have hoped for. She couldn't grow straight, not any longer.

She could survive.

"Well." Bertrice sat back, pulling her hand away. "We'll work on it, won't we?"

~

T hey did not work on it, not immediately. Bertrice had not imagined that it would be possible to make up for decades of pain in one afternoon, but she could feel the distance between the two of them like a yawning chasm as they packed up their picnic and beckoned the servant, who had been watching at a distance, to come take their things away. Clouds came and covered the sun; a fog crept in, and London returned to its typical winter gloom. Bertrice hired a cabriolet, which returned them to Violetta's room.

Still Violetta ignored her for the next hour, studiously reading a fading political circular, dated seven years prior. Bertrice couldn't forget the tree, the outburst. She'd been wrong. It wasn't the first time, and she didn't know how to fix it.

After an hour of near silence, Bertrice excused herself, claiming she had business with her solicitor.

And she did—there was always something or other that her blasted solicitors needed answering or signing or complaining about. That, though, wasn't the reason she had left.

She returned with bread and cheese and tea and milk three hours later.

Violetta looked up and smiled—a pale thing, lips pressed together and vaguely turned up—and nodded politely once, before returning her attention to the same four-page political tract she had been perusing hours before.

WORKERS, read the front page. *ORGANIZE, ORGANIZE, ORGANIZE!!!*

Bertrice raised an eyebrow. "You're involved in radical workers organizations?"

Violetta primly turned the page. "I am educating myself."

"Good for you." Bertrice watched her a moment longer. Even proper and prissy, pretending she'd not lost her temper earlier, there was an almost magnetic quality to Violetta. As if the roiling tempest she'd let loose had been caged—for now, and for now only.

Bertrice wanted to see it loosed.

But there would be time for that. In the moment, she wanted to make dinner. She laid out the loaf and the cheese, found the knife and a wooden board, and proceeded to chop things up.

Or at least, she *tried* to proceed.

It wasn't easy, mainly because Bertrice had never held a knife before.

Oh, she'd held paring scissors and butter knives and steak knives. She'd even held a little blade, one used to trim finger nails, for the space of five minutes.

But a knife? A *real* knife, with a serrated blade longer than her hand?

There had been servants for that. There had always been servants up until this exact moment.

She'd been so proud of herself, purchasing cheese and bread all on her own. Now she held the loaf in front of her, lifted the blade high—

"No," Violetta interrupted behind her, "*please* not like that. You must think of where your hand will be once the knife passes through the loaf. If you stab straight through that, the palm of your hand will be right *there*. Never use your flesh to stop a blade."

Bertrice wrinkled her nose. "I'm not an idiot. I would stop before then."

"Most of the time, I'm certain you would," Violetta said in a tone that suggested she was certain of no such thing. "But it's better not to have to rely on your skill. All it takes is one little mistake, and there you are, bleeding all over the bread."

"Hmmmph," Bertrice said, because it was becoming apparent she had no skill.

Violetta came to stand behind her, and ever so gently, she tapped Bertrice's knuckles. It wasn't sensual, but still, Bertrice sucked a breath in. "Here. Set the bread down. One hand to hold it in place. The other…"

Bertrice jabbed with the knife.

The knife lodged hilt-deep.

Violetta's hand stilled on hers. "Yes," she said after a long, drawn-out pause. "That's…definitely one way to start. Now that you've killed the bread, it's certain not to move about any longer."

Bertrice braced the loaf and managed to wrench the knife from where she'd buried it in the doughy deeps.

"So…like this?" She tried a motion as if she were slicing off a pat of butter.

"Maybe…" Violetta sighed. "More like cutting steak, less like cutting an apple? Slice. Don't push."

Bertrice tried again. Crumbs scattered like blood in an abattoir.

"Keep your hand steady, press straight down. Well. I suppose… that does serve much the same purpose. And it doesn't matter if it's jagged, once it's inside us?"

Violetta had made such smooth, pretty slices. Bertrice's bread fell apart in ugly, ragged, crumb-strewn chunks.

"Slice," Violetta said, and set her hands over Bertrice's. Her fingers were cool to the touch. But how could Bertrice possibly concentrate? Touches were rare in her life, except under the most impersonal of circumstances. Her maids had dressed and changed her with detached indifference; her doctor had methodically listened to her lungs and her heart; occasionally, a servant had brushed against her unwittingly in the hall.

Nobody had taken her hands with such gentleness since Ellie Nightwood had passed away.

"Like this," Violetta demonstrated. "See? The motion is all across; let the blade do the cutting, not your arm."

Even with instruction, the movement was unfamiliar. She felt as strange and clumsy as she had taking up needlework forty years ago, before the feel of thin metal at her fingertips became commonplace.

"You must think me a complete oaf," she said, after Violetta had guided her in chiseling off slices of cheese that looked as if they'd been hewn from rock by an inexpert stonecutter, and left her to bludgeon apples into shards.

Violetta glanced at her from her place at the fire, where she was turning the cheese toaster. Her lips pressed together; she looked into the sparking coals, as if seeing something that had long since disappeared.

"My mother didn't know how to cut, either."

Bertrice looked up from arranging her irregular wedges of fruit on two plates.

The other woman was still staring into the fire.

"She escaped the Terrors in France. She watched her own father die on the guillotine, disguised in servants' clothing at the edge of the crowd. She and my father fled in disguise. They came here. They had only the jewels sewn into her gown to sustain them. They were just important enough for the Revolution to target, but not quite interesting enough to gain entry to the top levels of English society." Violetta spoke evenly.

"I'm sorry." Bertrice had always been bad at showing compassion, but that seemed like a thing one should say at such times.

Violetta shrugged one shoulder. "I was born here. I never knew any differently. The money from the jewels ran short when I was almost an adult. There were no funds, not for maids nor cooks. My parents had no skills with which to earn a wage. My mother put a good face on it, of course." Another shrug. "It was easier for me to learn all these little things myself in order to make a penny stretch. And then it was easier for me to care for my parents than to try and educate them." A third shrug. "I ought to have married, but nobody wanted me, and the thought of men having their way with me made me feel nauseated in any event."

"Your mother must have been very fragile."

Violetta nodded her head. Still…

"No," she contradicted herself. "Maybe she wasn't. But strength is relative to situation, and she was pushed into a place where all her strengths—her confidence, her ability to order a household—became weaknesses."

Bertrice shut her eyes. "I married because my mother told me I would starve otherwise. She was not wrong. My father was the sixth son of an earl, and I was his second daughter. I would have no dowry. So I married the richest man I could find. It was the usual bargain—I served as his entry into polite-ish society; he provided for me as best as such a person could. But once we were married, he had his place in society secured and I still had need of his money, every day." She exhaled. "It was not an equal relationship. All the strengths that a woman needs to land a good match are unequal to the task of surviving that match when it goes sour. Sometimes I hate my mother for not letting me starve."

It was the first time Bertrice had spoken that aloud.

Violetta did not rear back in horror. Instead she shook her own head. "Sometimes I hate my mother, too. She didn't know how to do anything she had to do, and she didn't want to learn. Once the money ran out, she placed the burden of survival on me. She could have shown me how to hope, but instead, the legacy she left me was fear."

"Fear of violence." It was as close as Bertrice could come to talking about those dark years, locked deep in her heart.

"Fear of not having enough," Violetta whispered.

"Fear of not *being* enough, of sitting silent while others suffer in the exact same way."

For a long while, they didn't say anything.

Fear at seventy years of age was different than fear at seventeen. At seventeen, Bertrice had been walking down the so-called correct path, trying not to stray with all her might. Her fears had not been her own; they had been gifts from her elders. *They won't think you're proper if you do that. You might never find a match. Do you want to live in a garret alone for the rest of your life?*

Here was Violetta, living out the worst nightmare that Bertrice's seventeen-year-old self had harbored.

"If I hadn't married," Bertrice said, "I might have been you. I think of you, cozy in this room where nobody can touch you. I fear I could become jealous."

Violetta shook her head violently. "Do you think so? Do you think that just because nobody wanted me, nobody would touch me?" She didn't say anything more, but her eyes squeezed shut.

And no. Of course not. Bertrice knew men. They were opportunists, and what could be a greater opportunity than a woman nobody cared about?

Violetta went on. "You don't need to worry one ounce about what you will do when you're eighty and maybe ninety, with nobody to care for you. I think *all* the time about what I would do with your wealth. We met because I begged for a portion of it. Do you ever think about what we're doing now?"

"You refer to the geese?"

"And the chorus. And your Terrible Nephew."

Bertrice had tried not to think at all. She was having an adventure. She was trying to *enjoy.*

"Men inherit property," Violetta said. "Not fear. He expects *us* to be afraid. Don't you wonder what he might do to inspire that emotion in us?"

Bertrice exhaled. When she'd left on this adventure, she hadn't thought about what it would mean aside from a chance to do precisely what she wanted. She had tried to avoid thinking about the consequences. But even if she put it out of her mind, it stayed in her body, bringing heaviness to her limbs.

"I do," she said. "I do wonder. And..." Despite her bravery, there was always a tense expectation in her gut, one that counseled her to hide. She'd learned to push through it, but the worry never left. "And I *am* afraid. I just don't want to be."

"Neither do I."

Bertrice looked over. Women inherited fear, yes, but it was because women were expected to care. They were expected to look out for children and grand-nieces and servants, to fear for them if anything went awry.

Somehow, in the last few days, Bertrice had started to care about Violetta. To care was to be afraid.

"You know," Violetta said, pulling the toasted cheese from the fire, "I have no idea what I will do if he decides to attack me. He could hurt me, and I don't heal as swiftly as I used to." Her hands were trembling. "There's nobody to look after me."

Bertrice thought of Violetta's hands on hers, guiding her while she cut. She thought of the flush that had taken over Violetta's face as she'd led the choir. She thought of her friends who had passed away, Ellie Nightwood especially, and the empty cavern of her life. Ellie would have scolded her, if she had been here.

But when she tried to bring Ellie's face to mind to deliver that scolding, the image wouldn't hold.

Scold you for what? she imagined Ellie saying instead. *For mourning? For taking time? For missing me? I would never.*

Bertrice had been trying not to care for so long, but she cared so much. Of *course* she'd felt nothing. Of course she'd tasted nothing. She'd been too busy holding her own grief at bay to feel life as it went past. She'd made noises about seeking out a forty-year old to distance herself from the woman in front of her.

Here was life, gently reminding her that she could care again. That her grief was allowed, but so was her joy.

"Don't be silly," Bertrice said. "I'll look after you. I promise." She was surprised to realize that she meant it.

Violetta turned to look at her. She often looked as if she were seeing some point just beyond Violetta, and at first she did that. But then her gaze shifted to contemplate Bertrice directly, and Bertrice remembered what she had said earlier. *My eyes cross, no matter how hard I try.*

Bertrice met her gaze, reached out, and took her hand. "I promise," she said more fervently.

And for one bare moment, Violetta lit, blossoming at her touch, her eyes burning into Bertrice's with a radiant intensity. Then she sank back, pulling her hands away.

"Thank you," she said. Her voice seemed sad and small. "Thank you. But we have a contract, signed with herebys and everything." Her jaw squared. "And we have work to do. I don't need your promise." Her fingers clenched at her side, as if remembering that touch. "Let's take care of your Terrible Nephew. I'll take the money that's owed, and I'll…"

She didn't say what she would do, not for a long time.

"You'll…?" Bertrice prompted.

"I'll do what I've always done," Violetta whispered. "I'll survive."

CHAPTER SIX

Two weeks later

Violetta stood at the top of the staircase in the rooming house she definitely did not own, about to execute what was both the brightest and the stupidest idea that she had ever had in her life.

She was going to hell. The only question was which path she would take on her road to the inferno.

She was certainly going to pay for her misdeeds. The last weeks had been torture. Torture for the Terrible Nephew; in the days past, they'd pelted him with eggs and dusted him with flour. They'd left putrid cheeses outside his room, and coaxed goats upstairs, convincing them to eat his undergarments.

They'd also been torture for Violetta. She'd pulled back from Bertrice as much as she could, limiting their physical contact to the brush of a hand. Sometimes she could not help herself, and their eyes met in a blaze of radiation that took her breath away. In those moments, she felt like her want was leaking from her, incapable of containment. She wanted to be loved. She wanted to be desired. She wanted someone who saw who she was.

But every time she allowed herself to let her guard down, she remembered the truth. She *didn't* want someone who saw her as she was, not at all. She was a liar. She couldn't want to be seen.

And so every time, she yanked her hand away or cut her gaze to a corner of the room, and gathered her wanting back inside her.

Violetta didn't know if her destruction would come in the form of Mr. Toggert, who—despite his foolishly lengthy absence—would soon discover that she was altering the leases of his tenants.

Perhaps it would be Mr. Cappish who brought the authorities on their heads. In the past few days, on the strength of Violetta's nonexistent authority, Bertrice had convinced every tenant except the Terrible Nephew to escape the hellish landscape that had once been a peaceful rooming house.

Maybe it would be Bertrice herself. She'd promised to look after Violetta, but that wouldn't last, not once she knew the truth.

It was just as the vicar had promised when she was young. One little lie sent out roots and branches, burgeoning in madcap fashion until her whole life was blossoming with falsehoods. She was probably going to hell. She was certainly going to prison.

And, well. It seemed a very far-off thing. She could panic about it later. Imprisonment was a form of planning for her dotage, wasn't it?

"Up here," she called to the plasterer she had engaged yesterday. "The work is up here."

Beside her, Bertrice snickered.

Oh, her current plan would not buy food. It would not keep her from any of the punishments that awaited. It would not give her anything except a private, desperate joy, but when shelter and food faltered in the years to come, it would be a joy she could hold on to.

Years ago, Violetta had been tasked with combining two rooms into one more luxurious set of rooms. It was from that experience that this idea had sprung.

Now she had only to execute it.

The plasterer came to stand beside her, frowning.

"You want me to plaster over this door?"

The carpenter was already at work. He had removed the door from its place and had fitted in a frame to cover the gaping hole. He was now nailing boards to cover the frame he'd built to block Mr. Cappish's entry.

"Yes, that's precisely the work you were hired for," Violetta said. "Plaster over the door. Make it look as if there's no entry at all into the room."

The plasterer frowned. "But there's still a room, there? That seems wrong."

"Um…" Violetta tried to come up with a good explanation.

But Bertrice never let anything stop her, and Violetta adored that. She opened her purse and shook the contents, heavy coins rattling in place. "What *seems* wrong is that I'm paying you five shillings for two hours of work. One of those shillings is for your work; the other four shillings are for not asking questions."

"But—"

"The more questions you ask, the fewer shillings I pay."

"I do not think you understand. My worry is—"

"What in the devil's name are the two of you doing?"

The angry delight in Violetta's heart froze in place. She felt her breath catch in her lungs.

They'd been so focused on the plasterer that they'd entirely missed Mr. Cappish coming up the stairs. He rarely returned this early in the afternoon, but here he was, frowning at them.

Violetta swallowed.

Bertrice did not shrink back, though. "What does it look like?" she demanded. "We are plastering over the door to this room. Keep on, keep on."

"*This* room," Mr. Cappish sputtered. "You mean the door to *my* room."

"I mean the room that you have *no right to enter,* as you've not paid for the lodging in two years!"

Mr. Cappish took four steps forward to tower over his aunt. "You mean the debts that *you* have not paid, despite your moral, familial, and ethical obligations to me, your only living relation!"

Bertrice's fists clenched. "I do not owe you anything. Not *one* thing."

For one long moment, the two glared at each other.

Bertrice would hate the observation, but in that moment, Violetta could see a family resemblance in their eyebrows, thick and angry, their cheekbones, touched with pink. There was a similarity in the way they both straightened their spines and threw back their shoulders.

The Terrible Nephew reached out and set one hand on Bertrice's shoulder. His fingers clenched; Violetta's heart leapt inside her, while her thoughts scattered. She couldn't just stand about and watch. She had to—

Bertrice brought her cane around and smacked her nephew in the knee, causing him to buckle, curse, and grab the wall to stay upright. "Get out of here."

Mr. Cappish stood, leaning against the wall and rubbing his leg. He was no longer glaring. Now he was looking off into the distance, his eyes narrowed as if focused on some unseen goal. "This has gone on long enough. I have been patient—very patient. But you've had your fun, and this is entirely out of hand. I am the patriarch of this family, aunt, and I intend to exercise my rights. End this now, or…"

"Or what? Are you threatening me? Because I haven't started yet. I haven't *begun* to start. Must I advertise what you are in every paper in London? I will do so." She raised her cane again.

Mr. Cappish straightened and skipped out of the reach of his aunt's cane. "I have been decent to you." He spoke in stilted, polite tones. "In light of your advanced age, I have given you every kindness. But you are placing an utter *nobody* over your own nephew. It's not right." He cast a glance at Violetta on the word *nobody*, and a little chill ran down her spine. "I won't hear of it any longer. If you keep on, I will stop you."

"I should like to see you try."

"I shan't even have to exert myself." His lip curled up, and he turned to the two laborers standing at the door. The carpenter had frozen in place, hammer in hand. "Stop this work at once. This is my lawful abode; I do not give permission."

"She's in charge of the rooming house!" Bertrice said, pointing at Violetta, and Violetta felt her stomach turn, waiting for the inevitable. "And *I'm* the one with the money. *He's* not capable of anything except manning about mannishly, and that's about as useful as a tea kettle made of ice!"

"If you board up my lawful residence," Mr. Cappish said to the carpenter, "I will inform my friends at Glaser's, and we shall make sure neither of you ever work again. Now, who do you want to anger—these two aging nothings or a select group of men who control the workings of London?"

"I knew there was something off about this," the plasterer said, shaking his head. He packed up his tools. "I simply *knew* it." He was off, down the stairs, three seconds later.

The carpenter looked at his hammer, then at the frame, then at the hammer once more. "I'm sorry," he at least had the grace to say, before gathering his materials and absconding.

Mr. Cappish watched them go, a gratified smile on his face. "You see how it is, Aunt? They will *always* listen to me. I'm your only living relative. They can *sense* that, you know. You think you're so smart with your carpenters and choruses, but everyone else knows the truth. I'm right, and they'll always know it."

He was right. Oh, not in the sense that his actions had any real connection with "truth" or "right." But he was right in the most basic sense—in a way that Violetta had learned over and over in her life. Money and skill and ingenuity and diligence and creativity never won. Not when wielded by women; not when there was a confident man proclaiming otherwise.

But Bertrice did not seem to notice. "Every threat you issue," she said, "will result in further retaliation from me. I have gone along nicely my entire life. I am done."

"You?" He scoffed. "Gone along? *Nicely?*"

"Nice-ish," she amended.

He took a step forward. "Listen to me, and listen well. I will have you declared incompetent unless you write a cheque upon your bank for ten thousand pounds. Right now."

"If you need money, obtain employment."

His jaw squared. "*That* again. I told you, I'm a gentleman. I shouldn't need to labor."

Bertrice just smiled. "Let's see who issues the threats here after all. I suspect your fine club will toss you out on your ear if they knew the truth—that you have no money, no prospects, and a mountain of debts."

Mr. Cappish flushed betrayingly red for one moment, before stepping forward and pushing a finger into Bertrice's chest. "I have prospects. Immediate prospects. I have simply chosen not to pursue them out of the goodness of my heart. You're not invulnerable. Neither of you are."

Violetta was vulnerable—so vulnerable. She'd spent the last weeks playacting, pretending that she could be as brave as Bertrice. But she never had been. Mr. Toggert was going to find out. She was going to prison—or worse. Was this a felony? Would they put her to death? When the possibility had been hypothetical, she had faced it with equanimity. But now, now that the constables might be coming...

Bertrice smacked the floor in front of her Terrible Nephew with her cane. "Get out of here," she said. "Go on. Do your worst. You can't touch us."

"You've made your last mistake," Mr. Cappish said. "I will put you away forever. Both of you. Just wait."

Violetta felt her vision darken at the edges. She was dimly aware of Bertrice waving her cane once more. She could scarcely hear Mr. Cappish's footsteps sounding on the stairs, dim and distant compared to the ominous thump of her heart.

"Violetta?" The words came from a long distance. "Violetta? Are you unwell?"

She couldn't speak for a moment. She could scarcely breathe. For a second, she could think only of a crowd chanting for her blood—of the incredible parallelism of being killed in public, just as her grandfather had been—

"Violetta." Someone took hold of her hands. The touch of fingers was warm against the clammy coolness of her palms. "Violetta, dear. It's going to be all right. I promise. Breathe. Breathe."

She did her best, struggling to inhale before realizing that she needed to let out the air she had been holding first. Air. Air was good. Air was excellent.

"Violetta, dear. Listen. I won't let anything happen to you. I promise."

"I can't," Violetta finally managed. "You don't know—it's—I have *nothing*, Bertrice, and I'm going to lose it all."

"No, you won't."

It wasn't a promise that Bertrice could remotely keep. She *had* to know that. Violetta had tried. She'd tried to make herself safe. She'd tried to make herself strong.

And what had it done? It had led her here—to this moment. She'd lied to Bertrice. She'd *lied*, and now Bertrice didn't even know how far she had been led astray. Everything was going to go up in flames, and it was her fault. If only Violetta hadn't involved Bertrice. If only she'd been smart enough, clever enough, to think of a solution besides fraud. If only—

"You won't lose anything," Bertrice repeated. "I promise you, you won't. It will all be well."

It wasn't a promise that could be kept, and yet that mindless reassurance calmed Violetta anyway. Her heart seemed to return to its normal rhythm; her vision cleared.

She pulled her hand from Bertrice's, straightened her spine, and stared at the unfinished wooden framework. "What do we do?"

Bertrice looked determined. "Now? Now we go on the offensive."

Violetta blinked. "I thought we were being offensive already."

A tiny smile played over Bertrice's face. "Oh, no," she said. "We've barely even started."

CHAPTER SEVEN

I t took almost twenty-four hours for Bertrice to escalate her tactics. She'd had to visit her solicitors—an *entire* office full of men who believed it was their occupation to comment on all of Bertrice's plans with such frivolities as, "you can't be serious" and "you cannot really intend to *do* that" and other similarly depressing inanities.

What was the point of giving people *money* if they kept asking you *why*?

Eventually, though, her money prevailed.

"Are you sure about this?" Violetta asked, as they approached the park the day after her nephew had accosted her when she had been rightfully trying to board up his room.

Bertrice was *not* sure. All the more reason not to admit it. "I'm sure as sunrises," she snapped.

"Oh, dear." Violetta glanced over at her. "That's bad."

"Do you believe in sunrises?"

"It's London," the other woman said with a lift of her shoulder. "It's winter. Nobody can see the sunrise through the fog of a London particular."

"Well, then." Bertrice refused to harbor feelings of

uncertainty simply because it was logical to do so. "Pick a different analogy. What *are* you sure of? Death, they say, and taxes, but I can't see that either would make a productive comparison. What do *you* think you can count on?"

"Angry men getting their way," Violetta said dryly.

Damn. Bertrice felt her certainty slip.

"Pick something else," she said. "*This* evening, we're dealing with women."

And they were.

Normally, Bertrice preferred not to interfere with working girls—they had enough worries as it was—but when it came to relieving them of her Terrible Nephew's company, she felt as if she were doing them a favor.

It had taken a few questions and a few coins to discover his habits. Another handful of coins had guaranteed that a baker across the way would send a shopgirl to alert her when the Terrible Nephew emerged.

This late winter afternoon was near-dark, with a rolling greenish-black fog blanketing the park. Spindly, half-leafed trees seemed to come from nowhere, leaping out of the mist like phantasms.

She could hear the Terrible Nephew before she could see him—the grating, whiny tone of his voice seemed muffled at first, compared to the higher, clearer responses of his companion.

He was arguing. She couldn't make out what he was saying at first; his words didn't resolve into sentences until he was close enough to appear in the fog like a dark, shadowed, thing. He was standing too close to a cloaked woman who was trying not to look at him.

"Mr. Cappish. I have told you and told you again. The answer is no." The girl stood stiff-backed, her face tilted a quarter-turn away. She really *was* a girl; she could not have been older than twenty-four.

God curse Terrible Nephews the world over. Bertrice wasn't having it.

But the Terrible Nephew was not ashamed. "Molly," he was saying, "you're only saying *no* because you don't understand economics. What I'm offering is the same as saving—one puts money in the bank; it gathers interest, and your patience is repaid in a few years' time with a good return on your investment."

As they drew closer, Bertrice could see the girl's face. She was pretty, round-cheeked, and flushed red with something between fear and anger.

Molly narrowed her eyes. "Fucking you is like putting funds in a bank," she repeated dubiously.

"Exactly like that." He reached for her hand; she stepped away.

"Banks have money." Another suspicious look. "You don't. Get off already, won't you?"

He sighed. "In a few days' time, I shall have the means to be generous. Very generous. I will remember those who were kind to me. As I said, it's a simple matter of economics. Now, are you good at economics or are you poor at them?"

He set one hand on his hip and cocked one eyebrow as if this devastatingly terrible argument had proved some point. And maybe it had—just not the one he'd intended. Molly stared at him for a moment, as if she had no idea how to answer an argument that not only defied logic, but reason, sense, and propriety at the same time. Then she responded the only way possible: She burst into laughter.

"That," she said, wiping away tears of mirth, "is the stupidest thing anyone has *ever* said to my face. Are you sentient, man, or is your head made of bricks?"

"Well, actually," the Terrible Nephew said, drawing himself up, "it's funny you should mention bricks, because there's a well-known economic fallacy about construction material that I learned of in my Oxford days. Do you wish to be economically fallacious, Molly? I shall be kind and explain the whole to you. Suppose a man has a brick—"

So engrossed was he in his Oxfordian story of economic fallacy, that he did not notice Bertrice and Violetta approaching through the fog. Molly didn't look as if she needed saving, but honestly, it was kindness to interrupt.

"I will pay double your normal rates," Bertrice said, waving her hands from the five feet that still separated them, "if you will *not* engage in intercourse with him."

The Terrible Nephew turned to look at her. He let out a great sigh.

Molly, beside him, took the opportunity to put a few feet of distance between them. "You don't have to pay me, love. I've already said I'm not doing it."

"Aunt Bertrice," groaned the Terrible Nephew, raising a hand to touch his forehead. "You never learn, do you?"

Oh, they'd tried to teach her. Years and years and years, they'd tried to teach her. It gave her pride that she hadn't learned.

"He's my nephew," she explained to Molly.

Molly frowned. "Have you some religious objection regarding his immortal soul?"

"I'm fairly certain that whatever soul he was assigned decamped years ago. There won't be an angel in heaven willing to allow him entry once they get to the bit about how he claimed that fucking him is like putting funds in the bank. *If* they get there. He's done worse before. You *do* know him to some degree, yes?"

The corners of Molly's lips twitched. "I fucked him once before." A shrug. "He's fast, at least, but it's boring. I'm certainly not about to do it for free."

The Terrible Nephew gawped at this, then straightened. "I have explained and *explained*. It is like putting money in a *bank*, it is, and it's really, truly not my fault that women like you haven't the head to manage your own finances!"

Molly let out a louder guffaw. "Oh, is *that* what it is?"

"Robby Bobkins." Bertrice turned to him. "You have not been able to manage your finances since you were *thirteen*. You spent your inheritance from your mother in *five years*. You've been living on gifts from friends and credit you cannot repay for three. Why are you lecturing women about your inability to pay them?"

"How many times must I say it? Do *not* call me Robby Bobkins. My name is Cappish—Mr. Cappish. I once extended the offer to you to refer to me as my dear friends do, but—"

Bertrice leaned close to Molly. "Oh yes," she said. "He *did* tell me. His intimates call him 'Clappy.'"

Molly laughed harder. "I'll have to spread *that* one about. Lord."

"Here." Bertrice reached into her purse and took out a heavy coin. "That's for not fucking him. Please spread the word—not fucking Clappy here is like putting money in the bank, and I am the bank."

"It's *Cappy*, not *Clappy*. Aunt, perhaps you do not know, but when one says 'clap' in this particular con-text… It doesn't have positive connotations. It really doesn't. You might want to rethink what you are saying."

"What, in the context of banking?" Bertrice let her eyes widen innocently. "I hadn't realized. What could possibly be negative? Who *doesn't* want to clap when one visits banks?"

"Him," Violetta said behind her.

"Ah, right. He can't manage his funds."

"I don't know what you must think of me." Molly was staring bemusedly at the coin in her hands. "I didn't do anything. I can make my own way."

"Yes, well." Bertrice shrugged. "We women have to make up for the men in this world, don't you think? What has Clappy here ever done?"

Violetta flinched, and Bertrice could not help but recall their earlier conversation. What could be more certain than angry men getting their way? For a moment, she faltered. Just for a moment. Then she remembered. Oh, yes. Bertrice didn't *care* if it was impossible to prevail. She didn't care if foul men with good breeding almost never paid the price for their misdeeds. There had been too many foul men in her life—in everyone's life. She couldn't make all of them pay, but she had a chance to make *this* one do so.

"Aunt Bertrice," the Terrible Nephew said. "You have gone entirely too far. I warned you earlier that you had crossed the line. I must tell you that since last I saw you, I have visited a solicitor. As your nearest next of kin, I have no choice but to have you declared mentally incompetent. I have already filed the paperwork."

This was met with silence.

"Robby Bobkins," Molly finally said, dropping the coin in her pocket. "Your own aunt. How could you?"

He shook his head. "It's only a matter of time, now. Have your fun, Aunt Bertrice. Enjoy it while it lasts. Everything you do and have done—the flour, the geese, the plasterers—it all only proves my point. You are not capable. I don't need to wait for you to die; I'll be given charge of your funds as soon as the courts can see to it."

Bertrice refused to look at him. She stared instead at Molly, who looked back at her with something like pity.

"Have a nice day." Out of the corner of her eye, she saw the Terrible Nephew touch the brim of his hat and walk off.

She refused to watch him go.

It wasn't a surprise that he'd chosen this course of action. He'd always acted as if *her* money was really *his.* He signed fraudulent sureties in her name. He assured his fellow club-members that her fortune was coming to him. He even told women on the street that her money was like a bank. He was waiting for her to give in or die, and now that he realized that she had no intention of doing either anytime soon, he'd decided to make her wish she was dead.

"It was coming to this." Bertrice had known it deep in the pit of her soul, in the fears and nerves she hadn't wanted to acknowledge from the start. "It has *always* been coming to this."

～

Violetta had no idea why they needed chocolates, but Bertrice insisted, and she was not about to complain about being dragged to a chocolatier. She would not object to being made to inhale the seductive, luscious dark scent. She watched as Bertrice pointed to confection after confection on the chocolatier's counter, and when it seemed that the chocolates were overwhelming in number—an entire generous box of them—Bertrice turned to her.

"Which ones do *you* think we should add?" she asked.

Violetta had not had chocolate since she was a child. As a girl, these dazzling creations of sugar and gleaming brown cacao hadn't even existed. She remembered chocolate as something for drinking, and then only on special occasions.

For most of her life, it had seemed pointless to want chocolate. She could want and want and want, but she couldn't get it. Instead, she let herself yearn for prosaic things. She wanted a home, one she might stay in for the rest of her days, one that would be warm enough with gloves and a thick, wool blanket in the winter. She wanted the small joys: feeling sun on her face, or—luxury of luxuries—chicken soup on a cold day with doughy dumplings.

She could dare to want these things because they were within her reach. She did not know how to want glossy brown squares dotted with roasted nuts.

"That one," she said, jabbing her finger at the glass case at random.

"And?"

And?

She jabbed again, careless, and the shop girl followed her commands, until that generous box became a ridiculous pack that would have bought chicken-and-dumpling soup enough to last half the winter.

Bertrice just nodded from the side.

The shop girl layered light paper over the top and tied the wooden box with a bright blue ribbon.

"A gift," Bertrice had said, tucking it under her arm. Maybe that was her plan to defeat her nephew—to find whomever would evaluate her mental competence and bribe them with sweets.

It wasn't the worst plan. Violetta wished people

had tried to bribe her with chocolates at some point earlier in her life. She had thought herself moral and upstanding, when in reality, nobody had ever tried to corrupt her with anything she really wanted.

Instead, she swallowed her desire for a taste of sweetness. Easy enough; the knot of worry that Violetta had been holding in her stomach refused to untangle. Ignoring it had not yet made it better. It sat like a solid lump of brass, whispering the words that the Terrible Nephew had said.

It's been enough. It's been enough.

She had never been enough. Not to look at; not to bribe. The journey back to Violetta's room was accomplished in silence.

Violetta had spent all her life packed into that dull, sepia periphery of society. Living a careful life, one that was appropriate to her station. Now she'd shoved herself out onto center stage—carelessly, without any possibility of hiding behind the curtains. She had known perhaps from the first moment in Bertrice's parlor that it was all going to go horribly wrong. Now, her heartbeat seemed to encourage that final, inevitable doom with every thump.

But Bertrice did not seem to be bothered by the eventual outcome. She ascended the stairs to the building entrance the way she always did—slowly, one step at a time, but surely. *She* didn't seem to have the weight of the world burdening her shoulders; she carried only the weight of the chocolates she had purchased.

"Are you not worried?" Violetta asked, when they finally stood in her small room.

"Worried?" Bertrice wrinkled her nose as if this were the last thing she could possibly have considered. "Why the devil would I be worried?"

"Your nephew."

The nose twitched again. "We don't call him that."

"Your Terrible Nephew," Violetta amended. "You know, the truly awful absolutely no-good one who has filed papers to have you declared mentally incompetent? *That* nephew."

Bertrice blinked. "Him? Good lord, Violetta. I don't care what happens to him. Do you honestly believe I am supposed to be worried on his behalf?"

"Worried *about* him. Not worried *for* him."

"Oh." Bertrice looked as if the possibility had just occurred to her. "You think I should be worried about him? Oh, that's sweet. It really is. But dear, he's so *lazy*. What is there to worry about?"

"You have finally pushed him into action. Aren't you afraid?"

Bertrice removed her cloak and tossed it on a chair; Violetta hung it up for her, and when she toed off her shoes, aligned them as well. Bertrice sank onto the edge of the bed, still clutching the box containing the chocolates, with a sad little sigh. "No," she said, rolling her shoulders as she sat in place. "No, I'm not afraid of him."

"Not even a little?"

"The opposite of fear," Bertrice said, "is a plan, and I have a plan. So no, I am not afraid."

The definition of fear was someone *else* having a plan and Violetta having no say in it, even if that person was Bertrice. Maybe—if the last few weeks were any indication—*especially* if that person was Bertrice. "What's your plan?"

Bertrice set the box to the side. But instead of removing the ribbon, she reached into a pocket of her skirt and took out a piece of paper. She unfolded it from its square shape and handed this to Violetta.

Contract, it read, *for the sale of one (1) rooming house, located at...*

"To start, I'm going to buy your rooming house," Bertrice announced.

Violetta's vision blurred, then fractured. She inhaled and looked up, unable to read any further. Unable, even, to speak. Violetta *had* no rooming house; she had only her own too-threadbare lie. She'd not said a word, not as they went from bare acquaintances to friends to…to whatever this was. *Thump*, went her heart. This was how it ended. *Thump*.

"I can't." The words fell from her lips.

"You can't what?" Bertrice removed the box of chocolates and played with the ends of the ribbon holding the lid in place. "You can't sell it? I'm willing to pay two thousand pounds—more than its fair market value."

Violetta shook her head and pushed the document away. "Bertrice. It's not—" All their friendliness, all their camaraderie—it was all hollow if she did this.

But it was already hollow. And…two thousand pounds.

Oh, the things she could let herself want if only she had two thousand pounds! A little cottage in a village near the sea with an almost temperate climate. A garden; someone to see after her when she grew too old to do more than sit in her rocking chair and watch people pass.

The funds to give pennies to beggars, and pounds to girls on their wedding days…

She didn't even have to come up with a *different* lie; she just had to keep repeating the one she had already uttered.

"It's not *what?*" Bertrice asked, looking at her with that look that was not at all accusation.

"It's too much," Violetta seized on. "Too much— it's not worth that, you must *know* it's not worth it—"

"But aren't *you* worth it?" Bertrice's eyes speared her. "You've been of such immense value to me, Violetta. The world felt flat before you. I had *nothing* when you arrived, and now I feel…" She shrugged. "Well, I don't need to go further. I *feel* again, and I didn't before. Can't I repay you for that?"

"Don't." Violetta felt something like grief rise up in her. "Don't, please don't. I *can't.* I can't take this."

"You can't have someone see everything you've done and think well of you?"

Violetta choked, trying to swallow her sobs.

"You can't accept a reward for your hard work?"

She had waited and waited for someone to see her inner beauty. To value her for who she was. And when she'd given up and found Bertrice, she'd thought it was just her rotten luck to have finally missed her chance.

But now it felt like more than a missed chance. It felt like a tragedy.

"I can't sell you the building!" She almost screamed the words. "I'm not capable of doing so, because I do not *own* it. I have lied to you for weeks, and if the true owner ever realizes what we've done to his tenants, we shall both go to prison!"

Bertrice listened to this calmly. She didn't widen her eyes. She didn't gasp. She didn't scream for help. Instead, she gave a tug to the blue ribbon circling the box of chocolates. It came undone and slid to the floor. She opened the box, and the heady odor of chocolate filled the room.

"Here," she said, holding it out. "Have one."

"Did you *hear* what I just said?"

"That was a little dramatic." Bertrice shrugged. "We aren't going to prison, I don't think."

A possibility rose to Violetta's mind. "Oh—of course. You believed I owned the building. Likely, they'll let you off for that. I think." *She* would still be imprisoned, but that was almost inevitable. "I promise, I'll testify to that effect."

"Pooh," was Bertrice's response. "I knew you didn't own the building."

"I beg your pardon?"

Bertrice frowned into the box, and selected a dark brown oval. "I knew it," she said, "from the first day, because the maths didn't work out. You wouldn't be living *here*, without servants, instead of in the rooming house. You wouldn't be dressing like *that*, if you had that kind of property. You didn't have enough keys or enough money for this to make sense. I inquired of my solicitors. There's a register of who owns what and so forth. They found it out on the second day."

Oh. Violetta hadn't considered the possibility. She could scarcely fathom it now. Her mind felt blank.

"I asked my solicitors to look into it; they brought me the whole story. You labored for Mr. Toggert for almost fifty years and he sacked you to avoid paying you a pension. Typical story. Of course a man was at fault."

Violetta's head was spinning. She couldn't grapple with any of these revelations. There was one thing she could cling to. "You really shouldn't blame men for everything."

"No, just the ninety-eight percent of society's ills they're responsible for."

"That's—listen, Bertrice, that hardly seems fair. Men can't be responsible for *everything*."

"Now we're just quibbling over what a fair percentage should be." Bertrice shrugged.

Violetta tried again. "Bertrice, I *lied* to you. Recklessly. Wantonly."

"So? You have some point here, I assume."

Violetta had thought that it was enough to say that she lied. She gestured, almost angrily. "How can you act like it's nothing? It wasn't *nice*."

"Of course it wasn't." Bertrice looked even more baffled than Violetta felt. "We established that you were not nice on our first evening together. The word for people like you isn't *nice*. It's 'not massively wealthy.' I may be a cantankerous pain in the arse, but when someone explains a thing to me, I do try to listen."

The possibility that Violetta had been forgiven before she even had a chance to beg for it left her shaken. She fumbled for words. "Why didn't you say anything, if you knew all that?"

Bertrice shrugged once again and put the chocolate in her mouth. "I'm not stupid," she mumbled through a mouthful of candy, "and you had a good idea. No point embarrassing you when you'd already been treated so poorly. I purchased the building from Mr. Toggert myself, once I realized what we were about. Everything we did was perfectly legal."

"You were trying to buy the building from me, yet you'd already bought it? Bertrice, I don't understand."

One swallow, and Bertrice sighed. She suddenly looked more tired. "I was *trying* to give you money. In case…" Her hands twitched. She looked away. "In case my nephew succeeded in taking everything away. That way I would know you were safe and well. But here you are, being absolutely stubborn about it. Bah. I *told* you I had a plan, but *no*, you had to argue about it."

Everything fell into place so easily. The chocolates. Bertrice's plan. Violetta's own mistakes.

Bertrice wasn't confident; she was *scared*. And unlike Violetta, she hadn't conjured lies from the depths of her fear in an attempt to defraud someone else. No; she'd thought of Violetta first.

"Bertrice…"

"Oh, hmph." Bertrice tossed her head. "Don't take that sweet tone with me; what use is it? Have some damned chocolates."

"I thought you said they were a gift."

"They are. In part, they are a gift to myself, which is why I have eaten three of them. But they are also in part a gift to you, which is why I said 'have some damned chocolates.' It's a way of indicating that *you* are the person I am giving them to."

Here she was, being bribed with chocolate for the first time in her life, and Violetta couldn't even accept the terms.

"Why? Why me?"

"I see you, Violetta." Bertrice met her eyes, and Violetta could not look away. "You are brave and strong. You learned to stay silent because nobody listened, but you spoke as soon as you knew you could. You are like an oak—beautiful, every part of you. Your hands." She took them. "Your eyes." She looked into them. "You, Violetta. You."

These seemed like words about some other person—someone stronger, someone braver. Someone who had been more truthful.

"Bertrice. I…I can't?" Her voice ticked up, though, and Bertrice seized on her uncertainty.

"It's easy. Open your mouth and put a chocolate in."

The road to hell was surely paved with cacao. Violetta could not have said why she hesitated, but somehow, selecting one felt like the first step into something more honest and more frightening than the pretense she'd been engaged in. If she pretended to be worthy of the chocolate…

It was one piece of chocolate. Violetta was already going to hell. Could there really be any harm in allowing herself to be plied with sweets on the way there? No. No harm at all; just chocolate.

She examined the pieces carefully before selecting one—a candied slice of orange, vibrant as the sunrise, half-dipped in dark, shiny brown.

She took a delicate bite. The taste burst across her palate, citrus and sweet balanced with heady bitterness.

"So tell me," Bertrice murmured. "What is it you can't do? You can't let me help you? You can't assist me anymore in my quest with my Terrible Nephew? I don't think that's what you're saying."

It was too much. Violetta shut her eyes, but that made the sweetness on her tongue seem all the more intense.

"I think what you're saying is that you don't understand how anyone can care about you. And it's sheer cruelty that this world has made you believe that. I've cared about you from the moment you stepped forward and stood by my side."

Violetta opened her eyes to see Bertrice sitting next to her, her eyes round and soft, watching her with the most curious expression on her face. She didn't deserve it. She truly didn't deserve it, and yet—

The road to hell was paved with chocolate, and Violetta had already chosen her path. She leaned in and touched her lips to Bertrice's. She shouldn't. She *knew* she shouldn't. And yet Bertrice kissed back, leaning in with a soft sigh. The kiss was soft and brittle all at once—soft against her lips, soft in intentions, soft as if this were the start of a long journey. It was brittle because Violetta knew it was the end. Where could they go from here?

Bertrice had fought for Violetta, had pushed her

to this moment. She'd known about her lies, and when threatened with the loss of both money and freedom, had tried to make her safe.

What had Violetta ever done to prove herself worthy of such care? She shut her eyes, but she couldn't shut off her questions. She couldn't shut off the feel of Bertrice. Bertrice's kiss whispered against Violetta's lips with a gentle certainty. How could she kiss like that, as if the world didn't matter? How could Bertrice take Violetta's wrist, promising safety and stability, when Bertrice was still at risk?

And—ah—that was it. Everything slotted into place. Their hands intertwined, palm to palm, fingers winding about each other, clasping each other tightly even as Violetta knew they'd never been at greater risk of separation.

Bertrice was offering Violetta what she could not have herself.

This kiss—this sweet touch of lips and limbs—it whispered of all the things that Violetta had never allowed herself to dream about. Dreams of companionship were like dreams of chocolate—impractical, when she had to worry about more prosaic things like bread and coal.

Yet here she was. Bertrice's hand slid up her inner wrist, to her elbow, pausing at every inch. At the scar on her forearm, left in an accident with a jagged nail; at the wrinkles of her elbow; at the loose folds that the decades had made of her upper arm. Violetta felt as if her skin was paper—too easy to rip—and yet she also felt as if she were illuminated from within.

Every part of herself that she was supposed to hate—every fold of skin, every discolored freckle—Bertrice touched and set alight. Violetta had never felt so seen.

And yet this kiss was a lie. *You will be safe,* Bertrice promised. *You will be loved. You will be beautiful.*

Bertrice's fingers landed lightly on her hair, petting the gray curls, acknowledging them.

Violetta had taken so much from Bertrice. She had lied to her. She took this, too, this offered affection. She drank it in as if she were dying of thirst, and only these falsehoods could quench it.

The road to hell was paved with chocolate and kisses, and Violetta gave into her damnation. She gave back her own truth to Bertrice's kind lies, letting her know with her own fingers, her lips, and her tongue. *You,* she thought, taking Bertrice's head into her hands. *You, with your Hallelujah chorus singing madly in a world that prefers silence, you offering comfort to everyone who needs it and stealing it from those who don't*—you, *you will be safe.*

No woman has ever before prevailed against an angry man, but you will. You *will.* She sent back all the love and beauty she saw in the other woman.

You, her fingers whispered, running down Bertrice's neck. *You, you, you. You are beautiful.*

She could feel the strength in the other woman, the muscle and sinew that had survived all these decades. Years of experience and hardship sang to her. Here, in Bertrice's flesh, she could hear all the things that they as women could not bear to say to each other, but must carry with them anyway—all the wounds that had healed into hard scars, carried by the sex so often referred to as soft.

Another kiss, and another. Bertrice's hands slid around Violetta's waist, holding her close. Another kiss, until Violetta could think of nothing but the kisses. The kisses gave way to little gasps—ones that said that whatever other lies Bertrice told with her flesh, in this moment, Violetta was beautiful to her.

Nothing before had made Violetta feel so...grateful. So cared for. So seen.

It had been one thing to accept lies. Truth was too much.

Violetta tried to pull away. "I...I don't..."

Bertrice halted, her hands pulling from Violetta. Her eyes were unfocused for a second, before she looked into Violetta's face. "You don't want this?"

Violetta was near tears. "I don't *deserve* it."

"Violetta." Bertrice reached out and touched her cheek, and Violetta could not stop herself; she leaned into her palm. "Sweetheart. You deserve it. You deserve it all."

"I *don't*. You can't make a thing like that true just by saying words. When matters became difficult for me, I folded up my principles and I—I simply—"

"You simply went on," Bertrice said. "You refused to give up. You refused to doubt your own worth *then*. Don't do it now."

"But—"

"But don't take my word for it. Take your own. Deep down, you *know* you've done good things. So stop this nonsense right *now* and name one."

That direct tone caught Violetta up short. "I —well."

"*One* good thing, and don't tell me there haven't been anything."

"Well. I survived." It was all she had.

"Pah. So do cockroaches. So do eels. There's more."

"Before...before I was let go." Violetta swallowed. "I was good at what I did. I listened to people and helped make their homes comfortable."

"Yes, that's more like it. Keep going."

"I try to be compassionate when I can, and stern when necessary."

"Go on."

"I keep excellent records." Her voice sounded shaky. "I make cheese toast extraordinarily well." She paused, searching. "I...am good at identifying things I am good at?"

"No." Bertrice smiled. "You're remarkably bad at that. Do you not recall my needing to browbeat you on this very issue a mere minute ago?"

"Bertrice." Violetta leaned in and let her forehead rest against the other woman's. "You know that you're worthy, too? That you deserve comfort and safety?"

Bertrice gave out a little choked sigh.

And after that, it was easy to go on. It was easy to undo the buttons of each others' gowns, to kiss down bared shoulders, to lift up chemises—Bertrice's was edged in lace; Violetta's hem was bare—to show skin that was dusted with age spots and veined like the finest marble.

It was amazing how years of mere existence had taught Violetta to hate herself, as if simply existing in the impossible sea of society's expectation put hateful scales over her eyes and made her believe that her own body was unworthy of love.

Loving Bertrice—kissing knuckles that were swollen with age, running her hands up breasts that time had given a graceful sway—made those scales fall away.

Every act of gravity and time made beauty in nature—except when it happened to human women. Not any longer. Ravines carved in her forehead by time made a striking landscape. Grey hair between her legs made a gentle forest. Bertrice came to her, touching, exploring, telling her with every brush of her fingers that she *deserved* to be touched, *deserved* to be explored.

Bertrice's fingers pressed against Violetta's sex. She felt as if she'd been parched for so long that there could be nothing but dryness. But arousal came, and with it, moisture. Bertrice rubbed her thumb lightly against the lips of Violetta's sex, and then, when Violetta gasped and parted her legs, slipped her hand between them. Their kisses grew more frantic; Violetta's own hand went between Bertrice's legs, finding her wet, feeling her open for her. Each gasp felt precious. Each noise of encouragement made her feel as if she belonged, as if she were cared for, as if she were—

She came, arching her back, and Bertrice followed her down that path. Violetta was almost in tears as they leaned into each other. Bertrice felt warm and smelled sweet, and *oh*, it was such joy to feel this, and such sorrow to know it could be taken from her.

After they'd held each other a while, Violetta poured a basin of water; they cleaned each other. She couldn't think of tomorrow. She couldn't think of how to proceed.

"There," Bertrice said. "Don't you see? You deserve too much. You deserve everything."

"I…" Still she couldn't say it. She shut her eyes, unwilling to go along.

"I have always wanted to know what you would *really* do if you had my money. Come now; take a little of it."

If she took the money now, she would survive. But what about Bertrice?

"I'm going to give you two thousand pounds," Bertrice said. "There's a contract and everything. And…no matter what happens…" She trailed off. "I'll know. At least I'll know."

Violetta inhaled. "Why the chocolate?"

Bertrice just smiled at her. "I wanted chocolate. I could *guarantee* chocolate."

And I couldn't guarantee any of the other things I wanted, Violetta understood.

What *would* Violetta do if the Terrible Nephew won and the worst happened? If she had money, she could do anything. Buy a cottage. Purchase steamship tickets anywhere in the world.

The prospects for her old age were shifting from "certain imprisonment" to "cottage on the French coast."

She could have her safety, no matter what happened to Bertrice.

Bertrice was watching her. Violetta felt like a tree, rooted in a riverbank. She wanted to survive. It was a deep hunger; she felt her roots growing deeper still. She had always wanted to survive; now she felt that hunger growing. She didn't just want to survive; she wanted to survive with chocolates and joy and companionship.

"You have already given me too much."

"I haven't," Bertrice replied. "You gave me toasted cheese."

Violetta knew she didn't just mean toasted cheese. She meant everything they'd shared together—the joy of taking charge, even for a few moments. The pleasure of having a common enemy in the Terrible Nephew, and knowing that they were allies. The walks in the park and the moments when they'd been able to just be friends. More than friends.

Violetta didn't just want to *survive*. Instead of falsehoods about owning a rooming house, she wanted to promise certainty. She wanted to promise Bertrice that she could have security and companionship, that she would never be hurt or taken away to prison. She wanted to be able to deliver the things she most yearned for to this woman. But she didn't want to lie to her again.

"What are we going to do?" she asked instead.

Instead of sighing pensively or shrugging, Bertrice laid back in bed, a small, satisfied smile on her face.

"I bought the building," Bertrice said. "I will do exactly as I wish, and never mind what the Terrible Nephew says. Maybe he will stop me someday, but he hasn't succeeded yet, and I refuse to cede victory on the basis of his paltry threats. My lawyers will have something to say about those, I imagine."

There Bertrice was—sounding certain again, with her vulnerability hidden away. *I want this to be true,* Violetta thought. *I need this to be true.*

But that wasn't what she actually needed. What she needed was to do what she should have done from the start—open her eyes, look around her, and fight for what she deserved.

Violetta leaned forward and kissed the other woman's forehead. "Bertrice," she said, "if you buy a building you already own for two thousand pounds, you'll never prove you're mentally competent."

Bertrice shut her eyes. "Just let me be certain you're well, no matter what happens. That's all I ask for."

Violetta could weep. That was as close to *I love you* as she'd ever heard from a person who wasn't her parents.

"I have taken care of myself thus far," Violetta said. "I will take your chocolates. I will take as many boxes of chocolates as you can lawfully give me." She reached up and set the palm of her hand against Bertrice's cheek. "But I won't accept my freedom at the cost of yours."

It turned out that she could say *I love you,* too.

CHAPTER EIGHT

Violetta woke the next morning.

The curtains were open an inch and dazzling sunlight spilled onto the wooden floors. It wasn't the first light of the morning, no, not by that angle. It wasn't even the second light of morning. It was maybe as late as nine, and Violetta could not remember sleeping so soundly since...

Well, maybe that one day twelve years ago, when she'd allowed herself to indulge in a long day at the fair and had been sore all the morrow. She stretched surreptitiously—there, sure enough, unfamiliar parts of her body protested. One didn't notice how many muscles one had in the body until one *used* them. And how deliciously she had used them.

The events of last night felt like a dream, gauzy and insubstantial. Bertrice, offering her a ridiculous sum. Wanting to hold and protect her, and not knowing how.

Violetta had never won what she wanted. Not safety, not security. After all these years, she had started to tell herself that she didn't really *deserve* them. The idea that she might was new, so new that she could almost smell it in the air—bitter and comforting at the same time, like a candied orange slice dipped in chocolate.

A small smile touched her lips and she shifted in bed again, stretching each muscle, bit by careful bit, her shoulders first, then her arching spine, then her toes, extended to their length, then her arms, stretching, stretching—

Her fingers found empty sheets. They closed almost spasmodically and she turned, her eyes wide.

No Bertrice.

Violetta's room was small—a bed, a table, and a wardrobe were all crammed higgledy-piggledy together, anywhere that there was space against the wall. There was nowhere to hide. If Bertrice was not in sight, she was not here. She'd left, and all last night's promises, spoken and unspoken, were dust.

Violetta should have known. She should have— her fears rose up once more, and then, as she glanced around the room, came to a halt.

There—on the table. There was a note.

Violetta shut her eyes.

Of course there was a note. Bertrice had no doubt…gone out to…fetch bread?

The half-loaf from last night sat on the table, wrapped in cloth, giving the lie to that possibility.

There was no point getting upset before she knew what she was getting upset about.

Violetta stood. The air was cold, her rough nightgown too thin after the warmth of the blankets. The rough floor froze her feet, and the hairs on her arms prickled.

She picked up the note.

Violetta,

I have to attend to some pressing business. Your pres-

ence is requested in the park in front of Glaser's at three in the afternoon.

Hereby signed,

Bertrice Martin

P.S. Bring the toasty cheese making thing, would you?

Not one word of affection. Violetta shook her head. Not one mention of what had transpired between them last night. Of course she wouldn't commit such doings to paper. Still.

Hereby signed. That was how they'd finished off the first contract. Violetta could almost hear Bertrice in her memory. "'Hereby' makes it more legalistic," she'd said. Legalistic. After last night…

Doubt was an old friend; it often came to keep Violetta company when she was lonely. Of *course* Bertrice had left. Of course she'd changed her mind, and of course all those words last night about beauty and safety and whatnot were meaningless. It had been sixty-nine years, and still Violetta had not learned—not truly, not as she should. She sat here, stupidly making excuses that she knew were lies, telling herself there was a reason.

But Bertrice had been as desperate last night as Violetta had been. She knew what she'd been threatened with. She cared—she truly cared—and what had happened last night *meant* something so long as Violetta held that meaning in her heart.

Violetta stood up.

Maybe she *didn't* deserve happiness.

But she didn't have *nothing.* She never had. She had her wits, her stubbornness, and fifty-seven pounds in the bank. Maybe *she* didn't deserve to be protected—maybe she'd forfeited the right when she told that lie—but by God she would fight anyone who said the same of Bertrice.

She needed what Bertrice would have had in her stead. She needed a plan. She was going to fight, and she was going to win.

"I promise," she said to the empty room where Bertrice was not standing, "that I will take care of you."

~

The gentleman's club a few minutes before three in the afternoon was the site of much disturbance. Violetta had been sore that morning and spending the last four hours walking around would not help her on the morrow. But strangely—in the moment—she had never felt better.

She'd expected that Bertrice had arranged a confrontation at Glaser's. She'd arrived assuming there would be one. But the scene she found was beyond comprehension.

First, there was a fire engine—a dark, hulking metal thing of pistons and cylinders, with a smokebox rising from it. Dark hoses were coiled neatly nearby. Then there were the firemen—why were there firemen? Why were they digging ditches in the nearby park? Why weren't they wearing the Metropolitan Fire Brigade uniform?

That last was easy to answer. The brigade had only been formed a scant handful of years before, and it should not have surprised Violetta that private companies still existed. Their existence in *general* was not unusual; their presence *here* was a mystery. There was no fire. There wasn't even any smoke.

There was, however, a distinctive scent—a chemical, paraffin oil sort of smell.

And there was Bertrice. She stood in the center of

this ruckus, surveying the goings-on like a general. Her hair was done up in complicated white braids. She walked about, nodding at the ditches, sniffing the air.

Violetta clutched the sack she had brought—containing her cheese toaster and the warrant that she had spent the remnants of her money and the last few hours obtaining—and took a tentative few steps forward into the madness.

"Bertrice," she said when she was close enough to be heard over the din, "what is going on?"

"Oh!" Bertrice turned, saw her, and brightened. "Violetta! How good that you are finally here. Now we can begin."

"Begin? Begin what?"

"You should move back," Bertrice gave her a brilliant smile. "Smoke inhalation is bad for the lungs. Take care of yourself!"

"Smoke inhalation?" Violetta allowed Bertrice to draw her back to the iron railing by the Thames. "What smoke? There's no smoke."

"Oh, don't worry about that. There will be, once I set fire to everything."

"*What?* You can't be serious!" But as soon as Violetta said those words, she wondered why she bothered. Of course Bertrice was serious. Why not fire? "What will burning anything accomplish?"

Bertrice just patted the railing. "Promise you'll stay here," she said. The other woman drew a small pack of matches from her pocket; Violetta was too gobsmacked in the moment to stop her.

Bertrice couldn't mean to burn down just the rooming house, could she? It was next to the gentleman's club—*right* next to it. It was impossible to incinerate one without scorching the other. Besides, both buildings were made of stone. Stone didn't burn.

Did it?

But there was a little pile of what had once been furniture near the door of the rooming house, now chopped into kindling. She could make out legs, bits of drawers…

Bertrice lit her match, dropped it on the pile, and…*whoosh.*

The entire mess burst into flame, catching almost immediately.

Bertrice whooped and retreated as swiftly as she could with her cane, cackling. "Here it goes!" She made her way to Violetta's side, grinning madly.

Violetta's jaw dropped. "Dear God, Bertrice. What are you doing?"

"Well, I can't *win* against the Terrible Nephew, but I can still make certain that he'll lose. I can't *wait* to see the look on his face. I said I would get him out, and by God, I will. It's *my* building; I can burn it if I want to."

Violetta glanced over at her. The fire was growing; the door caught first, before the flames spread with a *whomp* that she could feel deep in her spine.

"It's stone," she protested. "Stone can't burn. Can it?"

Bertrice's mouth twitched. "The exterior is stone. The interior? There's wood girders, holding up each floor. The stairs are wood. The furniture is wood. The carpet is extremely flammable, when it comes down to it. I don't suppose the stone will catch, but the rest of it?" A shrug. "We'll see how well it does."

As if to highlight this, flames leapt from an upstairs window. Then—oh, dear God—fire burst from a window in the gentleman's club.

"Bertrice." Violetta took hold of her hand. "It's spreading! You didn't buy the gentleman's club!"

"On the contrary. Giving money to a gaggle of men turned my gorge," Bertrice replied. "But it turned out *they* didn't own this building either. And their finances were terribly out of order. I purchased the building and had my solicitor negotiate with them to end the lease." The corner of her mouth ticked up. "Among other things."

Another window pane burst, this time on an upper level, and bright orange flame streamed from it.

The fire had taken over the two buildings so swiftly it could hardly be believed. In the few minutes since the blaze had started, a crowd had gathered, oohing and awing at the flames. Violetta could feel the heat, pulsing against her in massive wafts.

"Bertrice, you can't just…burn down buildings!"

"Oh, that's why the firemen are here—to make sure it doesn't spread. They've so much less work now that there's a public act. They were happy to help. According to that fellow there, the park is a bit of a natural firebreak, and we're here on the Thames, with water present. It's quite safe."

Violetta gave her a disbelieving look.

"Safe-ish."

Indeed, the firemen were presently hosing down a bush twenty yards from the house, soaking it in water so that the fire stayed contained.

Violetta tried again. "Don't you think it's burned enough? You might ask the firemen to put it out, now."

"Ah, well." Bertrice shrugged. "That's the danger of a fire started with oil. Apparently, one can't just douse it with water and expect it to go out? There's some details there. I'm not truly sure I understand. But I will leave *that* to the experts."

"Bertrice."

"Give me this," Bertrice said. "If the Terrible Nephew is to take over everything, allow me this memory—of watching everything important to him burn."

"This won't convince a magistrate that you're mentally competent."

"Hmph. Only because they are men. If more judges were women, they would understand that it is a miracle we have not razed this city to the ground. I am as much in my right mind now as I have ever been."

They watched until the fire turned orange and ruddy, until the gray stone streaked black, and the black turned to gray ash. They watched until the window frames turned to cinder and fell to pieces. The heat slowly dissipated, and the noise of the conflagration dissipated from a full roar to a mere whisper against their faces.

Then Bertrice took Violetta's hand. "Come." She guided her forward.

Violetta balked, planting her feet. "What are we doing?"

Bertrice just grinned. "If I am going to set Glaser's afire, then we are going to make cheesy-toast over the smoldering remains. It's time."

What were Violetta's options? Refuse? There was no point; it had burned. There was no unburning, not now.

Why *not* make cheesy toast?

Violetta went. She and Bertrice found a smoking door, and set up the toaster over the blackened remnants of the once imposing entry to Glaser's. It didn't take long for the cheese to be good and toasted, and they swapped bites, feeding each other cheese that tasted of smoke.

"I can't say it's not worth it," Bertrice told her.

It was there, as they stood over the smoking embers, that he found them.

"Aunt Bertrice!" Mr. Cappish sounded utterly aghast. "What on earth are you doing?"

Bertrice cocked her head and considered her nephew. "You're not very observant, are you? I'm making cheesy toast over the remains of London's ninth most prominent gentleman's club."

"Aunt! That was my club. And the building next door—I *live* there. All my possessions are—" He made a disgruntled noise. "You can't just burn things down because you're a little angry about my personal choices!"

A *little* angry about his personal choices? Violetta considered hitting him with her cheese toaster.

Bertrice just shrugged. "Nobody was inside."

"It's someone else's property. Those buildings are not yours!"

"False. I bought them."

He frowned, struggling, before spitting out: "You can't just *burn* things! My club has a lease! People lived in that rooming house!"

"I bought everyone's leases! I negotiated with your stupid club to throw you out as a member and move away! They left this morning and they don't want you any longer."

This, more than anything, seemed to distress him. He put his hands to his temples almost despairingly. "You did what? *They* did what? What is *wrong* with you?"

"What is going on here?" interrupted yet another man, and Violetta looked up to see a constable arriving.

The Terrible Nephew pointed. "She did it! This crazy bat. She set *fire* to my gentleman's club. Just— ask her. Ask anyone!"

Bertrice narrowed her eyes. "There is some misunderstanding. I *own* these buildings. I have the deeds, I assure you." She tossed her head, as if she hadn't a care in the world.

The constable stared at her in disbelief. He looked around the park, at the fire engine and the gathered crowds, before looking back at her. "What has ownership got to do with anything? It's illegal to set fire to buildings even if you own them."

"Oh?" Bertrice straightened and bit her lip. "Is that so? I had...no idea." A frown passed over her face. "Oh dear. I will never hear the end of this. I did not consult my solicitors on that particular point; I assumed they would attempt to dissuade me. They often do."

The constable once again stared at her. His gaze fluttered down, then up, and he grimaced.

Violetta could not blame him for his discomfort. Bertrice spoke with the certainty of the wealthy and the accent of the upper class. Her gown was silk and lace; she positively dripped with an air that said she could not be touched. And elderly, wealthy women were rather hard to take into custody, even if they were admitted arsonists.

Alas; she was *clearly* an admitted arsonist.

"Well," Bertrice sighed, "I don't suppose it will matter. But I was burning down my Terrible Nephew's gentleman's club and rooming house because he threatened to have me declared mentally incompetent. You have to admit my reason was just. Or you would, if you weren't a m—"

Mr. Cappish took a step forward. "Sir. I should explain. I am her so-called 'Terrible Nephew.'" He chuckled, and tilted his head—a little gesture that seemed to shout *Listen to me; I am a man.* "And my aunt here has had the oddest notions in her head. You have to admit—setting fire to a building? It doesn't *sound* very mentally competent."

"No…" The constable trailed off.

Mr. Cappish smiled. He stepped next to his aunt and let a hand fall easily on her shoulder.

Bertrice twitched, pulling away, but he reached out and pulled her closer. "This is a family matter," he said in slick tones. "Release her to me, and I'll take care of it. If you would be willing to testify as to what you observed here today before a magistrate, we will put her away where she can't hurt anyone again. *Won't* we, aunt?"

"You—you—" Bertrice sputtered, but she was never at a loss for words. "Put me in his custody, and he will surely kill me. He *will.* You can't do it."

The constable hesitated. It wasn't much, but it was a moment, and Violetta only needed a moment. She gathered all her courage, all the promises she wanted to keep, and she stepped forward.

"Sir," she said. "I can make this simple for you."

The constable looked at her. Violetta *knew* what she looked like—an old, dumpy woman, grayish hair frizzled with age. Her eyes crossed in front of her. Her gown *wasn't* silk; nobody would ever take her seriously.

That was what they had wanted her to think all of her life.

"*You* can make this simple." The constable gave his mustache a suspicious rub. "How can anyone make *this* simple?"

"Like this." Violetta took a deep breath, and removed the receipts she had spent the morning collecting from her bag, along with the order from the court. "You cannot release Mrs. Martin into this man's custody, because he will not be able to take her. He has owed a great many businesses in the area for years. In order to facilitate collection, I have purchased one hundred and seventy pounds of his credit." His creditors had been delighted to get anything at all; she'd received a discount on his notes. "This morning, I visited a magistrate and obtained a warrant for the arrest of Mr. Robert Cappish. He is to be conducted to the Queen's Prison as a debtor."

Bertrice had told her that she'd already tried it— but that they'd dismissed her efforts, because she was a relation of the Terrible Nephew. Ha. Violetta was no relation, and she'd take great pleasure in holding him to account.

"What!" shrieked Mr. Cappish. "You can't do that! I'm a gentleman!"

"As the holder of one hundred and seventy pounds of his debt," Violetta said, "I assure you I *can* do this. Maybe a friend will take pity on you and arrange for your release?"

"But—but—*she's* my only relation!" Mr. Cappish said, pointing at Bertrice. "And you *can't* put me in jail. I'm a gentleman! *She* burned down a building!"

"Well." The constable bit his lip. "She *did* own it, after all. And I can't ignore a warrant—it's signed by a magistrate." He considered. "This is difficult. I believe I must put you *both* in jail. How's that?"

"You can't imprison me! I have to be at her mental competency hearing tomorrow," Mr. Cappish protested. "If I am not there, they'll dismiss it for want of prosecution!"

"Oh, no," Violetta said softly, shaking her head. "How sad. What an *unfortunate* side effect that would be."

Bertrice was watching Violetta, a soft smile on

her face. It was silly, but Violetta found herself grinning back. She shouldn't feel so proud of herself. Bertrice was going to jail. And yet...

"Violetta, dearest," Bertrice said, brushing her hand against Violetta's elbow before the constable could conduct her away. "Could you contact my solicitors? I'd be most obliged to have your help with this small matter."

CHAPTER NINE

The courtroom the next morning was nothing like Bertrice had expected from reading Dickens novels. There were no shady looking figures lurking at the edges, wrapped in dark cloaks, nor was it a chamber of dark musty corners and unknown smells. It was just a room with benches, sunlight filtering in from back windows. There was no audience save for Violetta, dressed in her best gown, sitting demurely in the back. Bertrice's own gown was some blue lace-and-silk thing that made her look like a demure little doll. ("That *is* the look you are trying to achieve," her solicitor had advised.)

She felt like a child. *Sit straight. Smile sweetly. Don't blaspheme. Don't burn buildings, not even if it is the most effective method of evicting your Terrible Nephew.* Bah. Boring.

She'd already paid an enormous fine to the Metropolitan Fire Brigade that morning to win free of the jail. It felt like insult heaped upon injury to have to bat her lashes and look appropriately wounded for the magistrate.

"If you had consulted me," her solicitor was muttering, "we could have avoided all of this without burning any buildings at all." He sat beside her now, that rotten no-good spoilsport.

The magistrate wore a white wig, but no spectacles. The only point that seemed to match a typical Dickensian description was the man who must be some sort of assistant. He probably had a proper name to match his status, something like "clerk" or "mid-overlord" or whatever these folk called themselves. He would likely bellow if he heard himself called an "assistant."

He looked to be about twelve years old to Bertrice's untrained eye. Then again, she was pretty sure that everyone below the age of thirty looked like an actual baby to her, so that didn't mean anything.

"In re Mrs. Martin," the magistrate read. "Mr. Robert Cappish, prosecuting."

A silence reigned in the courtroom, disturbed only slightly by the noise Bertrice choked back in her throat. *He prefers Clappy,* she wanted to say, *or Robby Bobkins...*

Her rotten no-good spoilsport of a solicitor was almost certainly right on one point: Insulting her imprisoned nephew in court was a bad way to make her case for mental competence.

"Well?" The magistrate said. "Present the case."

The lawyers for the other side—and how Robby Bobkins had managed to pay a solicitor, let alone the slack-jawed besuited fellow who passed for a barrister on the other side, Bertrice would never know —shuffled papers before one of them stood. Likely he'd been chosen for the extreme slackness of his jaw, the slackest of slack-jaws among them.

"Your Honor," this man said. "We...know what Mr. Cappish's case is, but we are unable to prosecute it at the moment, as our primary witness, Mr. Robert Cappish himself, is indisposed."

The magistrate frowned. "He's ill?"

"Ah…" The man winced. "He's…in…a state which does not allow his presence here."

Heavens. Bertrice stared at the man. He must have trained for *years* to be able to stretch the truth to such bounds.

"What state is that?"

"The state of imprisonment," Bertrice heard herself interject. At her side, her own lawyer flicked what was supposed to be a quelling glance at her. Out of the corner of her eye, she saw Violetta behind her, ducking her head and hiding her smile. She should be proud; what an enormously lovely thing she had done.

Alas. Bertrice would have to allow herself to be quelled. It wasn't as if she *knew* how court proceedings were supposed to go on. If she took Dickens as her guide, they'd go on and on for six generations, and she hadn't the patience for that. Two generations was enough.

"Ah." The lawyer for the other side flushed. "Well. As to that… Yes. That would be the state in question. We would like to move for a continuance, if Your Honor would be so inclined, until such time as my client has an opportunity to…ah…attend?"

The magistrate sighed and looked upward. "Your client has requested custody of his elderly aunt, on the grounds that she is not mentally competent and requires guidance from a sober, staid gentleman such as himself. For what is he imprisoned?"

"Ah. A delicate matter."

"For nonpayment of debts," said Mrs. Martin's barrister. "The woman who holds his notes is in attendance, I believe, should you need to ask any questions of her."

The magistrate nodded and steepled his fingers. He turned to Mrs. Martin. "Mrs. Martin, do you believe yourself to be of sound mind?"

"Yes," she said. "I am old, and I am possessed of decided opinions, but I do think they're reasonably sound."

He nodded. "And—forgive me for being uncouth, but I must inquire—you are very wealthy, are you not? I notice you have employed Botts and Forthwell in your defense."

"My husband left me with a fortune of close to fifty thousand pounds."

"And your nephew…?"

"Has been cut off, since he will not treat the women in my household with respect."

"I see." The magistrate nodded again. "I could dismiss this case for want of prosecution, you know. Is that what you want?"

"Ye—"

"No," the barrister sitting on the other side of her solicitor said, picking up on some clue in the air that she had missed. "It is *not* what we want. Mrs. Martin believes that her nephew has had an adequate opportunity to make his case. It was outlined in the briefs he submitted, and it's nobody's fault but his own that he's not here to establish further particulars. We've submitted as evidence the proof that Mr. Cappish has already entered a false security on behalf of his aunt. I think Your Honor understands the precise contours of his veracity."

"Yes." The magistrate turned to Mr. Cappish's lawyers. "Your response?"

"Your Honor, this woman is deranged. The word

we had of her goings-on yesterday involved arson and cheese toast. She cannot be trusted."

"Well," the magistrate said dryly, "I wasn't worried at all when you said 'arson,' but cheese toast, now, that's another story. How dare she be possessed of a fortune and burn her cheese toast."

Behind her, Bertrice heard Violetta make a small sound, not quite laughter, and she had to hold back her own chortle.

"I—Well, they're *connected,* you see, and it's not—"

"If all you have is hyperbolic stories about burning cheese," the magistrate said, "I believe we're done here. Tell your client that he's to pay his debts himself and to stop relying upon his aunt. Case dismissed with prejudice."

"With prejudice?" Bertrice leaned over and whispered in her attorney's ears. "That doesn't sound good. What does that mean?"

"It's not good," her lawyer replied, in low tones, "for Mr. Cappish."

She glared at him.

And—of course he did—he relented. "For your Terrible Nephew. It means he can't bring the case again."

"Oh." Bertrice said. "Oh."

She sat in place, hands clenching, almost unable to understand what it meant. She had won—not just a battle, but an outright war.

She'd won, and she hadn't been alone.

~

fter she took her leave of her attorneys, there was nothing to do but wander about London in a daze, Violetta at her side. They found a path along the Thames and walked. A cold breeze blew in over the water.

"This isn't over," Bertrice said. They weren't touching; it was too cold to remove gloves, and holding hands through two layers of wool felt odd.

"No?" Violetta glanced over at her. "I thought that was what 'dismissed with prejudice' meant. That it was over."

She sighed. "One of his horrible friends will give him money, perhaps. Just because the club voted him out doesn't mean that someone won't take pity on him."

"Perhaps."

"Or perhaps Parliament will finally pass one of those debtor's reforms that it keeps promising to consider and he'll have to stop moldering in a cell."

"To be fair," Violetta said delicately, "I personally think that debtor's prison is uncommonly cruel. I wish they *would* pass those reforms."

"Me too." Bertrice sighed. "I hate having political principles. And once he's out, he'll start scheming again. If it's not him, it will be some other person. It never truly ends. There are always men."

Violetta glanced at her. "To be fair," she said once again, "that judge who summed up the entire affair in about three seconds of glancing at the evidence was a man. They're not *all* bad."

Perhaps. Perhaps they were not all bad. Bertrice considered the possibility. Her consideration lasted two seconds. "That's like saying that not *all* rats are invasive pests," she replied. "I can't tell if the ones who *aren't* attempting to enter my home and eat my food stores respect my private property or if they simply haven't had the opportunity. I don't wish to inquire as to the difference."

Violetta just shook her head and smiled. "Well,

take it as you will. But there's hope. Men may make up the police, the courts, the lawmakers. They may be husbands and brothers and nephews and uncles. Their voice may always be louder than ours."

"That's your version of 'there's hope'?"

"Yes, because despite all of that, we've discovered that we can be happy." For some reason, Violetta blushed. "If we're lucky, we may have decades of happiness left, still. Maybe men are all bad—I won't grant you that, but *maybe* they are. But if they are *all* terrible, then they are also so incompetent at ruining women like you and me that there is always hope. They can't take our joy away, and they've tried."

Bertrice bit her lip.

"They've had seventy-three years to defeat you," Violetta said, turning to her. Her eyes were wide and dark, and she was almost certainly the dearest thing that Bertrice had seen in years. "What do you think it means that they've yet to accomplish it?"

She looked upward. "It's only because I had *you* that I won this time."

"And it's only because I had *you* that I believed I could make a difference."

Their path along the Thames intersected the remains of the rooming house and the gentleman's club. The burned buildings looked dismal. Stone streaked black with smoke, dark gaping holes where there had once been wood window frames—it would take a while to restore them.

The park was a little disturbed—the firemen had, in fact, dug up a bit of it to be certain the fire didn't spread—and the girls in the park were clustered together, talking.

Bertrice frowned. There was something wrong with that, there was. It took a moment for the answer to arrive, and as it did, she grimaced. "You know, Violetta, I have made mistakes."

Violetta looked at her. "You, admitting it?"

"I have *all* this money," Bertrice said mournfully, "and I utterly *wasted* it burning down the ninth most influential gentleman's club in all of London."

"Good heavens." Violetta looked at her. "I can't actually believe you're admitting it. I do have to agree, it was...fun while it lasted, but arson is probably—"

"There are *eight more of them* out there," Bertrice interrupted, "bastard strongholds of masculine stupidity that they are, and I went for number nine. What idiocy! What ineffectiveness!"

Violetta threw her head back and laughed. "I should have known. Please, consider that one arson per week may stretch my meager limitations."

But Bertrice hadn't taken her eyes off the girls congregating in the park. Molly, hadn't that been her name? And others. The gentleman's club had burned down, and men were the police, the magistrates, the lawyers, and the lawmakers.

"No," Bertrice said. "Why burn them down, when there are so many better ways to set fire?" She started off across the way. The park, on closer inspection, was far the worse for the wear. The grass near the fire was singed black; slightly farther away, it was merely scorched at the tips. The women looked up as she approached.

No point beating around the bush. "Here now," Bertrice said. "You—Molly, yes? Have we altered your income?"

Molly stared at her, and then looked around the park, empty of men, and sighed. "It will all work out, I'm sure. We'll just have to make some adjustments."

Bertrice pressed her lips together, considering.

"Would you want to learn a respectable trade, if someone offered you the money to do so?"

Molly shrugged. "I *know* a respectable trade, but what with the new machines, lace-making hardly pays the coal bill in winter."

"Huh." Bertrice should not have been surprised that the newspapers were all wrong when it came to ladies of the night—or of the late afternoon, as these women might have been called. Newspapers were generally written by men; why *would* they understand women? "And what if I offered to hire you?"

Molly's eyes narrowed suspiciously. "To do what? I don't want any charity, and I'm rather tired of making lace."

"Look," Bertrice said, "here's how it is. I have a great deal of money, and I'm trying to get rid of it before my nephew inherits it. I've tried to give it to parishes and the like, but they've not used the money in a manner I approve of. What would *you* do if you had thirty thousand pounds to do good with?"

Molly choked. "To do *what* sort of good with?"

"Why are you asking?" said one of the girls near her. "Who would say no? I'll take it, if she doesn't want it."

"I don't know," Bertrice said. "I don't *know* what to do with it. But here I am, with too much money and too few real relations to leave it to, and here you are, with a temporary lapse in gainful employment. If I gave you access to thirty thousand pounds and said that I wanted you to make this world a better place for women—any women—what would you do?"

Molly frowned. "I would have to consider. It would be a huge responsibility. I don't know what you wanted to hear—likely not that—so—"

"Exactly that," Bertrice said. "You're hired. I shall

pay you…three hundred pounds a year to get rid of my money? Is that sufficient?"

"Oh my God." Molly shook her head. "This is a dream. Or you're lying. I don't *want* charity."

"It isn't charity. You are going to make it so that when my Terrible Nephew gets out of debtor's prison, which he undoubtedly will in truly terrible fashion, there's almost nothing he can inherit. It will make my life immeasurably better, believe me. Now, do you accept?"

"I'm not an *idiot*," Molly said. "I only stopped making lace because I can do arithmetic, and this is by far a better offer."

"Then," Bertrice said, holding out her hand, "we have a deal. I'll have my solicitors draw up the whole thing."

~

T he way back to Violetta's apartment seemed different. Next to Violetta, Bertrice was smiling and humming something—Violetta rather thought it was an off-key version of the Hallelujah Chorus. But despite those outward markers of happiness, there was…something to her stride. Maybe it was the way she gripped her cane. Maybe it was the fact that she'd just agreed to give away a huge portion of her fortune.

Maybe…

"Now that that's out of the way," Bertrice said briskly, in an almost business-like manner, "I suppose we should visit my solicitors and get you a cheque. I feel the need to pay you back for what you did today, at a handsome return. Two thousand—no, five thousand pounds. Have you decided what you want to do?"

Violetta turned to her. "Bertrice."

Bertrice just gave her a weak smile. "There are so many options, you know. You could get a cottage on the coast. Or purchase the building where you live." Her smile brightened. "Buy the building where Mr. Toggert lives, and add a flock of geese to his life."

"*Bertrice*," Violetta said, with a little more emphasis.

Bertrice seemed not to notice. "Or, I don't know. You could do anything you like."

"I don't know if I can do *anything* I like," Violetta said. "Am I allowed to stay with you?"

There was a long pause. Bertrice flushed pink, two little spots on her cheeks, and exhaled slowly. "Well. I wouldn't have wanted to assume that you'd... want that sort of thing."

Violetta had to hide a grin. "There's a vast difference between assuming and trying to send me off to a cottage on the coast. And I don't think you have to *assume* that I want that sort of thing, since I very much enjoyed myself every minute I was with you. Especially what happened two nights ago; I hadn't thought I was terribly shy about letting that be known."

"No," Bertrice said. For some reason this made the tips of her ears turn red. "I suppose not. But... you do understand, after you get that cheque, and after we figure out the commitment I've made to the women in the park... I'm not going to be all that wealthy. I did just set fire to some of my property."

It was obvious that Bertrice seemed to think that this might be a problem. The way she looked at Violetta—through her eyelashes, holding back just a little, as if waiting for rejection—was adorable.

"Oh, no," Violetta said. "I have spent my entire life

chasing the wealthiest people possible, and alas, I have been stymied at this final moment."

"I'll just have thirteen or fourteen thousand pounds," Bertrice confessed.

"Shame," Violetta said, "I suppose you'll only be allowed to buy thirteen thousand pounds worth of love from me. That's a real tragedy."

This had the intended effect. Bertrice turned to her. Her hands fluttered on the word *love;* she bit her lip, considering. "How much is thirteen thousand pounds worth of love?"

"It's sold by the weight."

"How much does love weigh?"

"Nothing," Violetta said, "which is very inconvenient for the seller who intends to make a business purveying it to the general public. Damn my poor business sense. If only we had someone at hand to explain how bricks worked."

"You're...teasing me," Bertrice said.

"And doing a fine job of it," Violetta told her. "Listen to you, you goose. I'm not sure which is worse—your belief that thirteen thousand pounds is a mere nothing, when it is in fact a ridiculous fortune, or your belief that your wealth is why I have come to care about you. I love you because you never let your fears stop you. I love you because your heart is soft—at least, to people who aren't men—and kind. I love you because when I was at my most desperate, you gave me choices instead of tossing me out. I love you because you're beautiful, and because you make me feel beautiful. I don't know why you think your money would factor in."

A slow smile spread over Bertrice's face. "Well. If that's the way it is, let's go home and have some more of those cheesy toast things."

Violetta sighed. "Bertrice."

"Violetta."

"Bertrice, you know that's not how it's done. I put my heart out into this cold weather, and you just demand cheese toast? You can do better."

"Oh, well." Bertrice sniffed and adjusted her collar. "I love you, but I've been terribly obvious about it. *Now* can we have cheese toast?"

EPILOGUE

A home in Boston, one and a half years later

Violetta came back from the market with a loaf of bread and a bouquet of bright yellow crocuses, fresh from the spring market, to find Bertrice poring over a letter.

"Bertrice?"

Bertrice looked up. "Vi, darling. Aren't those lovely?"

"Yes—are you crying, Bertrice?"

"No. Why would I do a thing like that?"

"I see little tracks of moisture on your cheeks."

Bertrice straightened, swiping at her face. "Nonsense. I've just had news. You know how we were worried because the Terrible Nephew was to be released from Debtor's Prison?"

"Oh, no." Violetta stepped forward, coming to sit by Bertrice. "Never say he's out. But he hasn't found us, has he?"

"No," Bertrice said. "But he went to my former bank and gave them a forged cheque, which he claimed was on my account."

"Oh, *no.*"

Bertrice's smile curled upwards. "Oh, yes. And they fetched a constable on the spot. Right back into prison. How glorious."

"What an oaf."

"Ten years, my solicitor writes. Hard labor. What utterly lovely news."

"Isn't it, though?" Violetta smiled, and felt one last, lone worry dissipate. "Let's eat in the sunshine, shall we? It's such a beautiful day."

They packed up sandwiches together, before heading across the street to a park. Boston was lovely; Violetta had found her old friend, Lily, and they had restarted their friendship. Now they both had friends to spare.

The park, when they arrived, was pretty—trees with pale, spring-green leaves dancing in the sunshine. They laid a blanket on a bench and sat, enjoying the warmth.

"So," Violetta said, after they'd finished their sandwiches, "why *were* you crying?"

Bertrice sighed. "It's going to sound stupidly sentimental."

"Oh no, not sentiment."

"I was just thinking how glad I was that you came my way. That's all." Bertrice spoke gruffly.

Violetta found herself smiling. She reached out and took the other woman's hands. "That's all?" Her heart soared. "I think you mean, that's all I could possibly have wanted."

"Nonsense." Bertrice gripped her hands back and smiled. "You should want everything. Let me manage dinner tonight. I know just the thing."

Captain Grayson Hunter knows the battle to complete the first worldwide telegraphic network will be fierce, and he intends to win it by any means necessary. When he hears about a reclusive genius who has figured out how to slash the cost of telegraphic transmissions, he vows to do whatever it takes to get the man in his employ.

Except the reclusive genius is not a man, and she's not looking for employment.

Amelia Smith was born in Shanghai as a child and was taken in by English missionaries. She's not interested in Captain Hunter's promises or his ambitions. But the harder he tries to convince her, the more she realizes that there *is* something she wants from him: She wants everything. And she'll have to crack the frozen shell he's made of his heart to get it.

~

(Unedited excerpt from somewhere in the first few chapters)

Captain Grayson tilted his head, and Amelia's eyes were drawn to the length of his neck—dark skin, firm Adam's apple, covered by a messy cravat of dark blue. "There's a Frenchman named Viguier who has made his own version of Morse code for Chinese characters. It's awkward and inefficient. When I showed it to your brother, he laughed and said you had him beat since you were eleven years of age. He told me something of the scheme. I want you."

The Captain couldn't mean it like that. He didn't mean that he wanted her, even though the way he looked, the way his eyes flashed dark, made a shiver run down her spine. He merely meant that he wanted her mind. Still, her heart crept up a beat.

"That's ridiculous." Amelia shut her eyes. "You're looking for a telegraphic expert. You've been misled. My brother and I, we played a child's game."

"Then *you* are the lucky one who will grow rich from a child's game."

She licked her lips and tried to be serious. "I don't want to grow rich."

"Fair. What do you want? To marry Mr. Pale? His mother's not much, but I assume he has charm enough to make up for it."

Amelia flushed. "That's not his name. And I wouldn't know. I've never met him."

Captain Hunter froze in place. She'd surprised him, she realized. His eyes widened and he stared at her.

Amelia turned away from the condemnation in his eyes. "Don't look at me so reprovingly. I'm a woman who fits in nowhere. Who will have me as I am?"

"Mrs. Smith."

She couldn't let herself listen to what he would say. "I don't want to hear your empty statements. I have my attractions, I know. I have a sturdy constitution. I have a good heart. I am kind, I am hardworking. I *know* that I will be an excellent helpmeet." Even if some parts of the business had not appealed to her, not the first time.

"Mrs. Smith."

"My parents took me in," she said. "They found my mother at the side of the road during the Taiping Rebellion. She was starving. She'd been displaced from her home, and I was an infant. She begged them to take me, and they did. They raised me as if I were their own. I *know* I don't belong here, but here I am, and I must try to fit in where there's a place for me. There's little enough of one."

"Mrs. Smith," he repeated, more softly.

"They believe in me," she said. "They want this for me. I don't wish to disappoint them."

"Mrs. Smith." Captain Hunter said one final time. "You've told me only what they want. What do *you* want?"

She knew precisely what he was asking. She could

feel the jagged corners of her wants, ready to slip out the moment she let them do so. Amelia shook her head. "Every girl has dreams. Every woman learns to pack them up."

Instead of acquiescing, his eyes flashed. "That is quite possibly the worst thing I have ever heard. Men never have to pack up their dreams—not the white ones, at any rate. Why should *you* have to?"

"I'm not white."

He ignored this. "Look, I came here expecting to negotiate with the brilliant Silver Fox as to terms of employment. I had in my mind maximums that I would agree to, depending on whether this Silver Fox met my expectations. But I see I will have to change my negotiation tactics. Here is what I am offering you: You may ask for three things."

"What, like conditions in a fairy tale? Like the moon on a string?"

"Exactly like that," he said. "In addition to a salary, I will give you three wishes. The only condition I place on your wishes is that you have to truly want them."

"You can't mean that. I could wish for anything."

He rolled his eyes. "Yes, you'd think so. But I'm an excellent negotiator, and here's the thing—I know there's little danger of that. Before you are able to wish for anything, you will first have to learn to wish for *something*. I'm going to get your practice wishes, and they'll hardly be difficult to deliver."

"Oh? And I suppose you're an expert at wanting."

He took a step toward her. His voice dropped. "I am."

She could feel it in the dark, deep pull of his words. There was something about his voice, gravelly and low, that made her chest squeeze. The sheer desire was like an undercurrent, threatening to pull her beneath the surface.

"I want to build the first worldwide telegraphic network," he said. "I want to own the means of communication. I want every word that anyone wants sent to come through me. I want them to pay me, and I want to be able to tell them no."

She swallowed.

"I want my family to never have to worry about…" He shook his head. "About anything. I want to take this world and rearrange it so that nobody can ever overlook me. I will do anything I need to do to get there. And that means that I intend to get you."

She swallowed at the vision that rose up at those words. For a second, she imagined them closer, wearing less. His hands sliding worshipfully up her thighs—No. She had to stop this. Employment. He meant employment. Of course he meant employment. But that jagged box of want inside her squeezed just a little.

"I know it's a hard choice." There was a mocking note to his words now. "You could labor in subservience to a man you've never met who will never see you as your equal. Or you could come work for me, and have someone who wants to hold the world in his palms to owe you three wishes."

Click here to find out more about *The Devil Comes Courting*.

OTHER BOOKS BY COURTNEY

The Worth Saga

Once Upon a Marquess

Her Every Wish

After the Wedding

The Pursuit Of...

Mrs. Martin's Incomparable Adventure

~coming soon~

The Devil Comes Courting

The Return of the Scoundrel

The Kissing Hour

A Tale of Two Viscounts

The Once and Future Earl

The Cyclone Series

Trade Me

Hold Me

Find Me

What Lies Between Me and You

Keep Me

The Brothers Sinister Series

The Governess Affair

The Duchess War

A Kiss for Midwinter

The Heiress Effect

The Countess Conspiracy

The Suffragette Scandal
Talk Sweetly to Me

The Turner Series
Unveiled
Unlocked
Unclaimed
Unraveled

Not in any series
A Right Honorable Gentleman
What Happened at Midnight
The Lady Always Wins

The Carhart Series
This Wicked Gift
Proof by Seduction
Trial by Desire

AUTHOR'S NOTE

Violetta refers to herself as a "surplus woman" early on in the book. This isn't a term (or a situation) that I invented. Throughout the nineteenth century, the problem of the "surplus woman" was discussed. Surplus women, of course, were women who never married (because apparently women only matter if they're attached to a man?), and the societal pressures introduced by Britain's expansionist colonial policies made them a real concern at all levels of society. Men from the lower classes were more likely to enlist in the army, and either die in combat or spend long years in situations that wouldn't support having a wife and family. Men from the middle and upper classes were sent abroad for colonial administration at a higher rate, and when they were around, found that most of their needs were met more easily by prostitution (which was at an all-time high at the time) and servants. The result was a large class of unmarried women who found that they had to be self-supporting in ways that prior generations were not.

If you were wondering whether words like "idiot" or "vile" make a contract less legally binding, the answer is no. If you are wondering whether words like "hereby" make a contract more legally binding, the answer is no. It doesn't matter how informal or formal you are. If you want to know what *does* make a contract legally binding, you can go to law school and read about chickens, multiple ships all hilariously named "Peerless," and other exciting content. (You probably should not go to law school for this reason, just ask me on Twitter.)

I also have a brief mention of the Metropolitan Fire Brigade. The history of fire in London is actually pretty awesome. Before 1866, fire protection was mostly managed by the insurance companies, and people who weren't insured, and didn't have money to pay a fire brigade, would watch their houses burn down. After several terrible fires, it became clear that this was not a workable solution in a metropolis the size of London. By law, the Metropolitan Fire Brigade created a public firefighting apparatus. That being said, I was able to find several references to private fire brigades in London after the creation of the Metropolitan Fire Brigade, and so feel that it would be reasonable for Bertrice to be able to pre-emptively hire one.

There are two minor events in the book that were inspired directly from outside influences. One is the reference that Violetta makes early on, that eating cheese toast supposedly makes one dream of Lucifer. I discovered this courtesy of author Theresa Romain (we both have an interest, both historical and contemporary, in cheese and toast) who alerted me to an 1848 review of *Wuthering Heights* by Emily Brontë. The review says: "There is an old saying that those who eat toasted cheese at night will dream of Lucifer. The author of *Wuthering Heights* has evidently eaten toasted cheese." Never let anyone tell you that authors didn't get bad reviews before the internet, and honestly, this is real review goals for me right here.

The other minor event is the point in the book when Violetta and Bertrice plan to plaster up the door to the Terrible Nephew's room. I got this idea from a book I read probably thirty years ago, called something like *The Legends of Caltech*. My sister went to Caltech and brought this back to amuse us. It did!

There's a major event in the book that was directly...anti-inspired from outside influences. I wrote just about everything about the Terrible Nephew before Kavanaugh's confirmation hearings. At the point when Kavanaugh's accusations surfaced, I had written it so that the Terrible Nephew was imprisoned by framing him with false accusations. After the hearings, some of those lines—particularly the ones about angry men who sexually assaulted young women getting their way—started to land with a different force. Kavanaugh and I both clerked for the same judges, and I'd been publicly outspoken in my criticism of him (both before and after the nomination). I didn't want anyone to think I was implying that Dr. Christine Blasey Ford was a liar, or that lying about sexual assault was appropriate if the person was undesirable enough. I had to rework a lot to make it go.

And just in case anyone was wondering, I really don't think arson is a great solution to any of the world's problems. Please don't do it.

One problem with writing happy endings in a world that seems increasingly irrational is that it is harder than ever to convince myself that they are realistic. But I nonetheless continue to do so. They haven't managed to win, not in the long term. They have all the money and all the power, and still, here we are. Happiness is not just an act of optimism—it is an act of defiance.

ACKNOWLEDGMENTS

Thanks to Rawles Lumumba, Rose Lerner, Lindsey Faber, Melissa Jolly, and Louisa Jordan for their hard work on this book. Thanks to my coven of brilliant women who share the same superhero origin story— being bitten by the same radioactive spider—and to my friends, who have put up with a lot from me, and who make me feel like I'm a reasonably valid person even when I'm pretty sure I'm not.

Also thanks to my husband, who listened to (many of) the jokes I made about men in this book and laughed. I've written several dozen books that share the premise that men can be genuinely decent people, and he helps me continue to believe this.

Sometimes I say more at the end of my acknowledgments about the process of writing books, et cetera et cetera. This is not one of those books where I have something cogent to say.

Instead, I would like to thank you, my readers. I don't just mean the usual "thank you for reading my books" and so on. I've heard from so many of you about how you strive to make the world a better place for everyone.

Thank you for everything that you do. Thank you

for being engaged and active in your communities. Thank you for the million ways you make people's lives better around you, both large and small.

Finally, thanks to my dog, Pele, who is fluffy and healing. Here's a picture, in case you have doubts.

Made in the USA
Monee, IL
29 February 2024